Dokkodo

by

Miyamoto Musashi

 All the illustrations in this organizer were created by Midjourney artificial intelligence, the perfect union between ancient culture and the latest technologies.

Miyamoto Musashi was a philosopher, artist, strategist, writer, lordless samurai and the most legendary master swordsman in Japan, where he is considered an honorary title Kensei given to warriors whose skill borders on perfection and which could be translated as "saint of the sword". sword. Towards the end of his life, Musashi wrote the book of the five rings and the Dokkodo, the book of the five rings is a work that, although it revolves around fighting and strategy, also contains timeless principles that are intended to symbolize processes of struggle and mastery in all fields and interests of life.

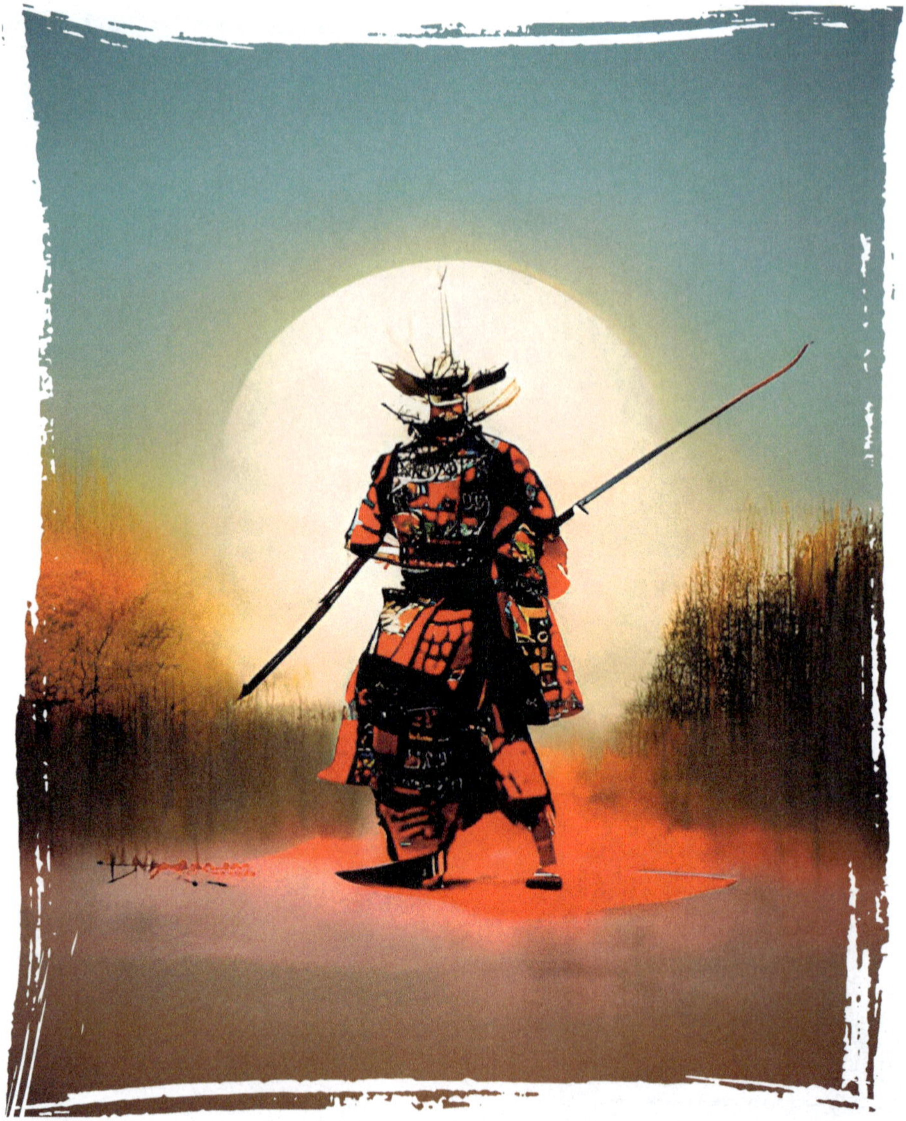

謹賀新年

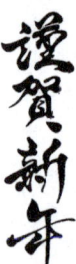

¨Perceive what cannot be perceived, pay attention even to the little things, do nothing, that is of no use¨. The Dokkodo he wrote a week before his death brings together his 21 principles for an honest disciplined and meaningful life. Later we will see the principles that we have thus bequeathed to us, but first let us know a little more about his fascinating life.

謹賀新年

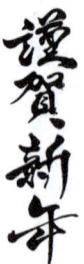

He was born in the spring of 1584 in the village of Miyamoto, his mother died giving birth and his father was a respected warrior who devoted himself body and soul to the arts of combat and whose prowess was so remarkable that he was named ¨He Ho Shou ¨ -the one who has no rival-, wanted to teach his son everything he knew, however, the relationship between the two was very tense due to the indomitable character of little Musashi.

When he was only seven years old he was expelled from home, from that moment he lived with his uncle Döring who had also been a warrior, but who had left that life behind to become a Buddhist monk and dedicate his days to study and meditation. Musashi grew up in a small Buddhist temple where he learned to read and write, he studied ancient Buddhist texts with his uncle, he delved into meditation and began to develop his spiritual life, however, he did not forget his warrior vocation and continued to train daily alone in the forests of the region.

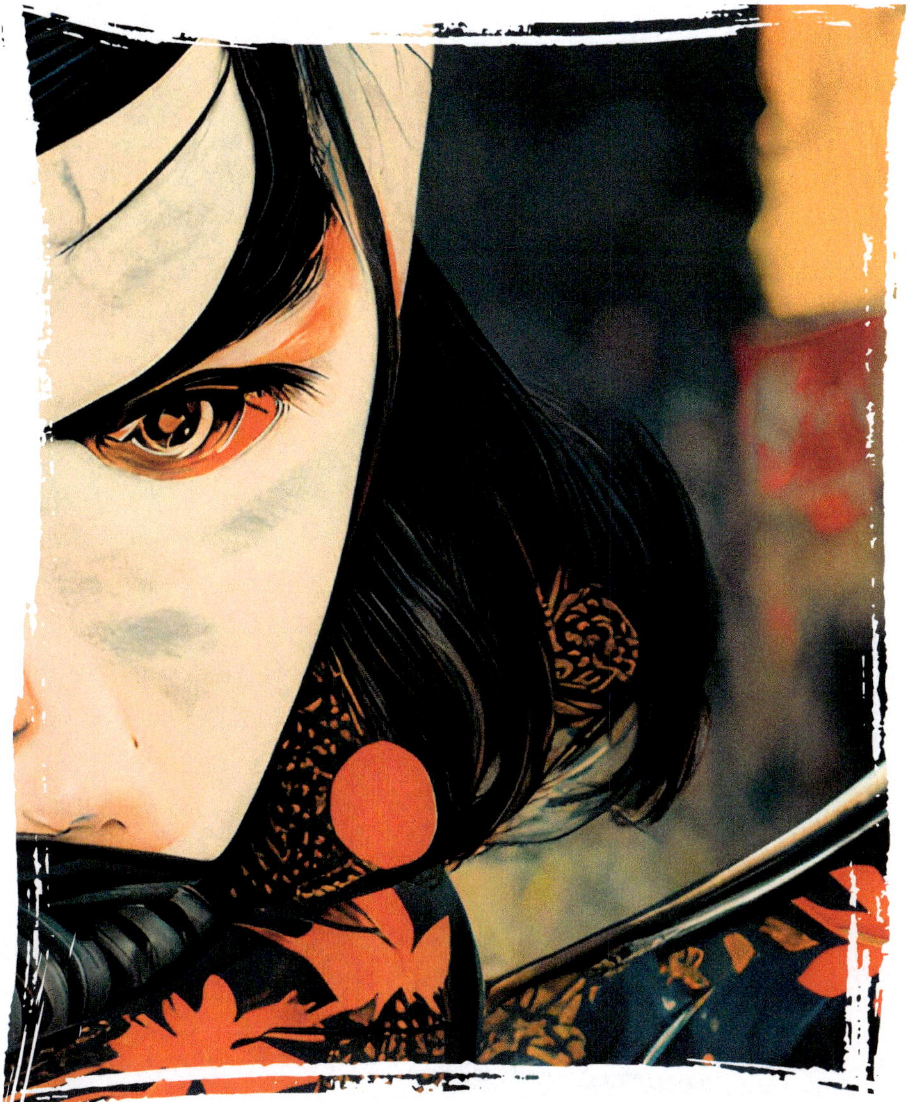

謹賀新年

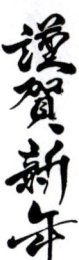

In the book of the five rings Musashi states that he had his first fight at the age of 13 against Arima Kihei, who had placed a sign by the river challenging any warrior to a duel, when Musashi wrote his name on the sign accepting the challenge, Kihei did not take him seriously as he judged the young Musashi as inferior and unworthy and his mistake cost him his life.

謹賀新年

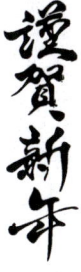

Three years later, he left his uncle's home behind and began a pilgrimage throughout Japan until finally, he met his father again, who was participating in a war between his lord Yoshitaka, feudal chief of Nakatsu castle, and the locals of the island of Nakatsu. Kyushu. Musashi joined the battle and fought alongside his father, after the victory Musashi knew that he wanted to continue exploring that life, he decided to become the best swordsman, defeat the best masters, and then found his own school to pass on his legacy to those around him. They would like to follow this path.

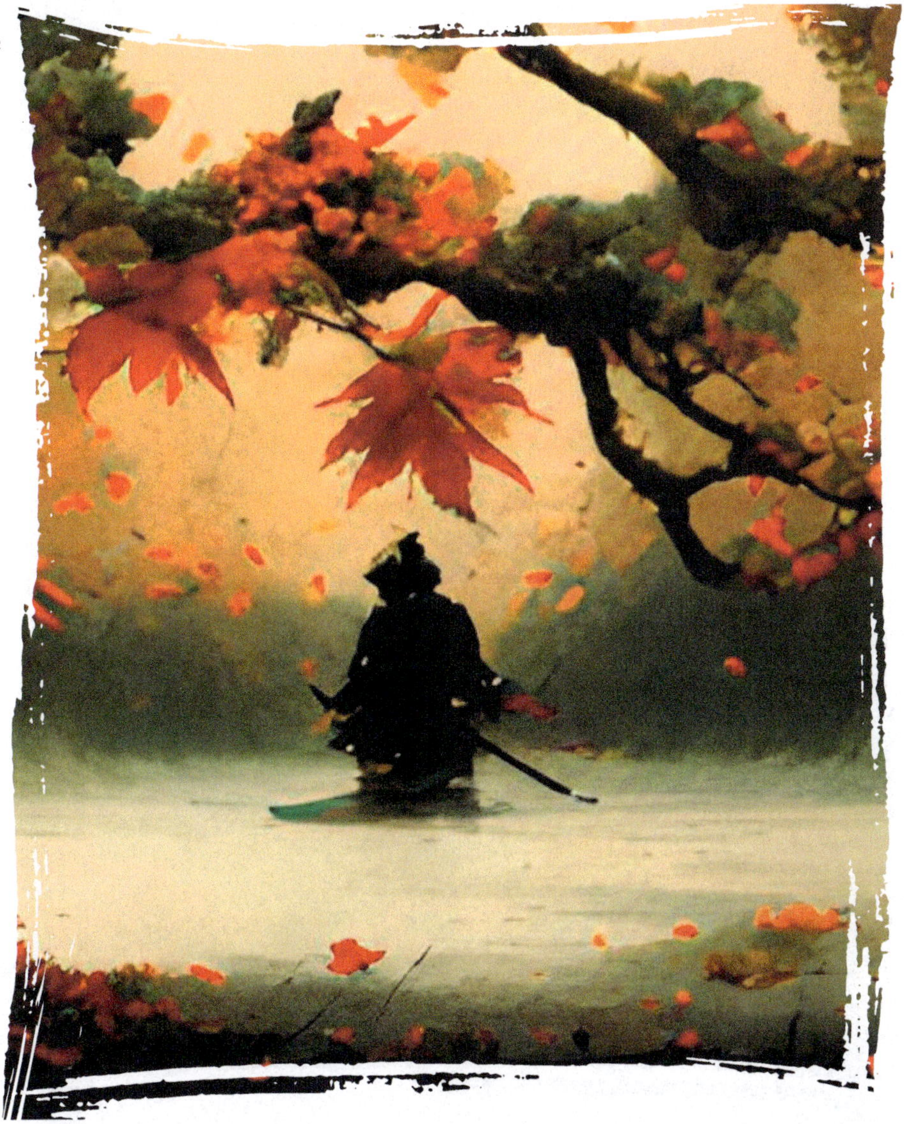

謹賀新年

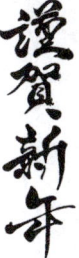

He wanted to hone his skills and dedicate his life to it without letting distractions get in the way. Moderation, discipline, sacrifice and not getting carried away by pleasure. "There is nothing outside of yourself that can allow you to become better, stronger, richer, faster, or smarter. Everything is inside. Don't look for anything outside of yourself. ¨

謹賀新年

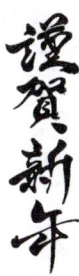

His next step was to challenge Yoshioka's school in Kyoto, one of the most respected centuries-old clans in Japan, his best swordsman Seijuro accepted the duel. Musashi used a bokuto, a wooden katana that in the West is usually known as a bökken, in just a few seconds Musashi finished off his opponent, after which Seijuro's brother, Densihiro, challenged Musashi to a death match, the result was the same.

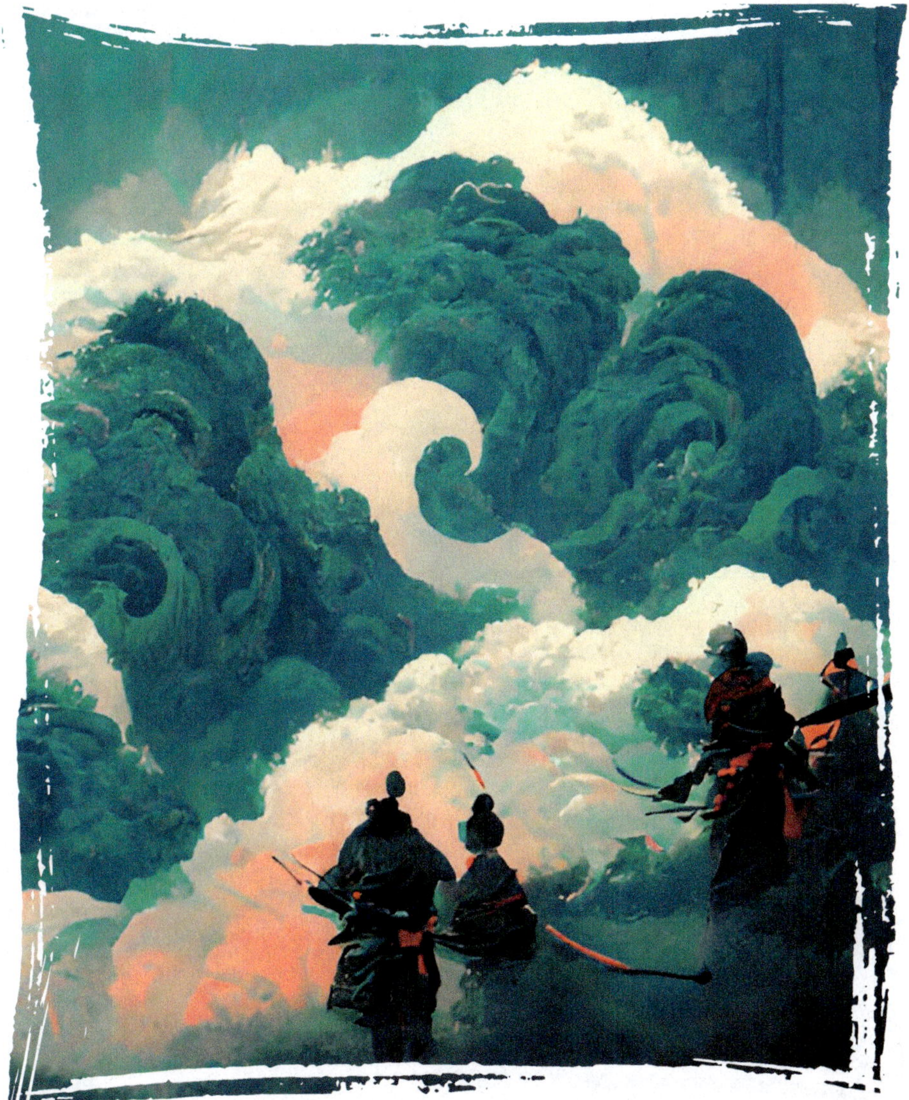

謹賀新年

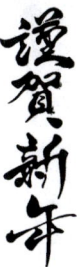

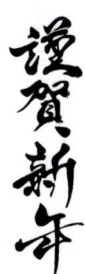

Between the ages of 13 and 29, as he himself tells us in the book of the five rings, he defeated more than 60 opponents in hand-to-hand combat. His last duel was on the island of Fukushima against Sasaki Kojiro, a famous master warrior feared throughout Japan. It is said that while Musashi was sailing to the island, he used one of the oars to carve a wooden sword with which he defeated Kojiro.

謹賀新年

He rejoined his father who had opened a Dojo in Kitsuky and worked there for the next three years, until his father died at the age of 85. Musashi received the letter from a former student Mizuno Katsunari, the Tokugawa and Toyotomi clans. Katsunari had entered the war, he was going to join the Tokugawa clan to fight and his 16 year old son would fight with him. He wanted Musashi to be part of the personal escort of the young warrior, Musashi accepted and it is said that in that battle all those present could see the impossible feats of this sword saint.

In 1640, Hosokawa Tadatoshi daymio of Kumamoto offered him a job as an instructor of his two-sword style that Musashi had developed over the years and brought him even more popularity. There he began to spend more time in the mountains of Iwao in an attitude of contemplation and meditation. He found a cave that seemed perfect for its remote location and the solitude it provided and in that cave he began to write his thoughts.

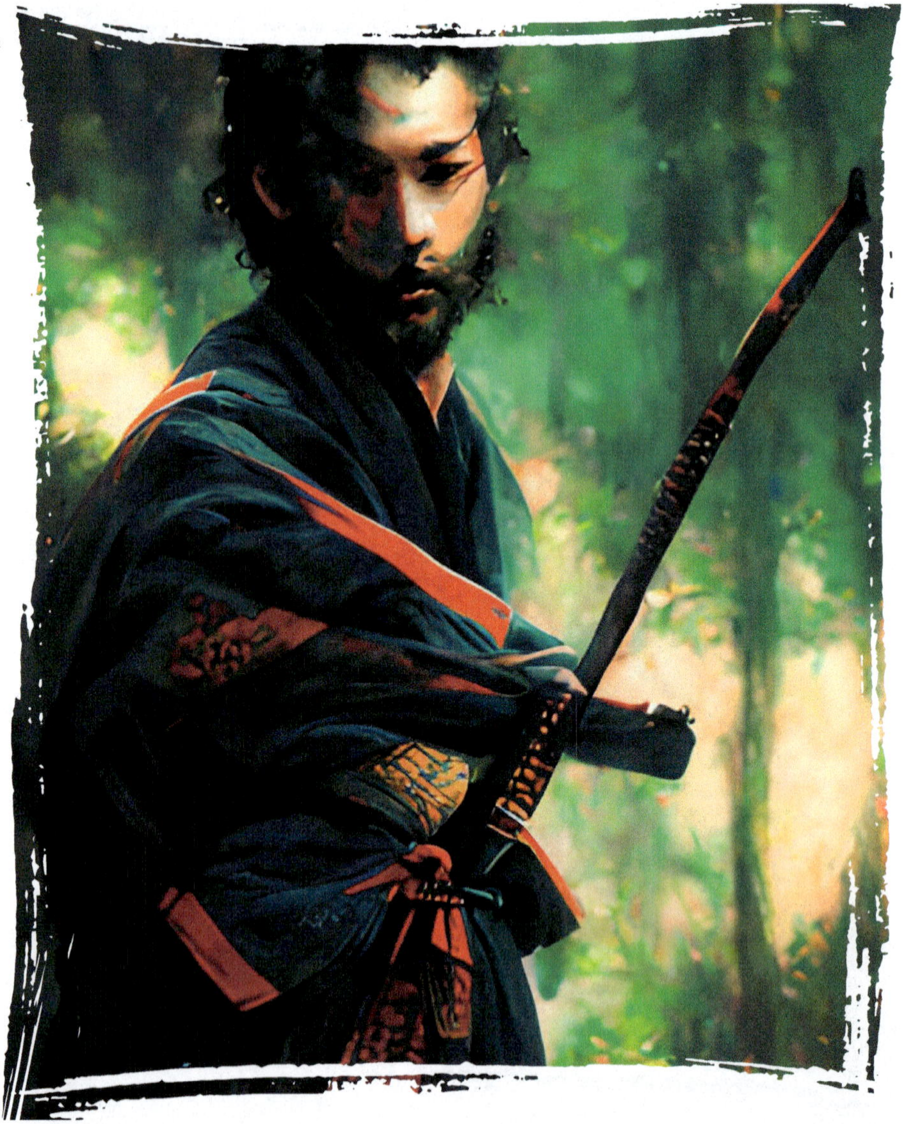

謹賀新年

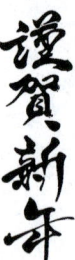

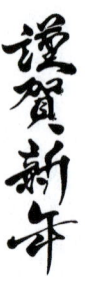

"Efficiency and continuous progress, prudence in all matters, recognition of the true value of different levels of morale, installation of trust and consideration of what can be reasonably expected and what cannot, all these are matters that the teacher has in mind."

謹賀新年

In the spring of 1645, he completed the manuscript of the book of the five rings, although it contains everything related to military science and the art of war with many references, highly technical aspects such as the guards, the rhythms in combat and the forms striking with the katana and the Wakizashi, his work also reveals the wisdom of a man who throughout his life learned to remain with an immutable spirit in any situation.

"Leave your spirit clear and open, putting your intellect on a vast plane. Diligent polishing of the intellect and spirit is essential. Once you have used your intellect to the point where you can distinguish what is true and what is not in the world, where you can say what is good and what is bad, and when you have already experienced several domains and you can no longer be fooled at all by people, your spirit will have been imbued with the knowledge and wisdom of the art of war.

The Book of Five Rings contains two main principles that Musashi approaches from different angles. The first is to remain internally calm and clear, even in the midst of violent chaos. The second is not to forget the possibility of disorder in times of order when life leads us to war and our minds are agitated, we know how to calm it down, when life leads us to to peace and our mind wants to settle in laziness we know how to keep it sharp.

¨With an open and direct spirit, neither tense nor too relaxed, keeping the mind centered so that there is no imbalance, fully savor that moment of tranquility, so that relaxation does not stop even for a moment. Although you are calm, your spirit is alert; though you are in a hurry, your spirit is not in a hurry. Pay attention to the mind, not the body. Do not allow there to be insufficiency or excess in your mind, even if you have a weak spirit on the surface, remain strong inside.

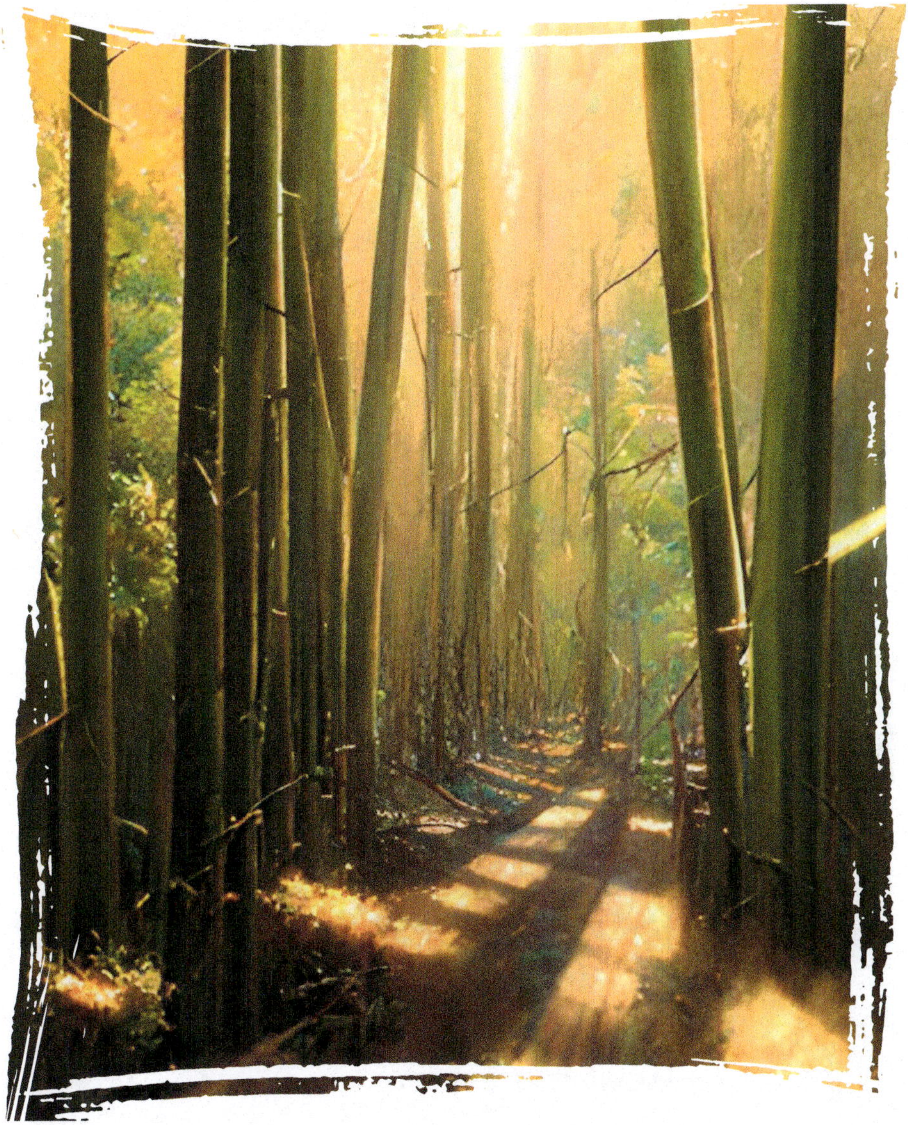

謹賀新年

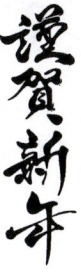

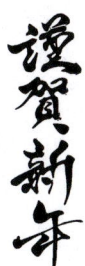

The five rings or five spheres as it has also been translated, refer to the five aspects that Musashi focuses on in his book, each one represented by an element, Earth, water, fire, air and emptiness.

謹賀新年

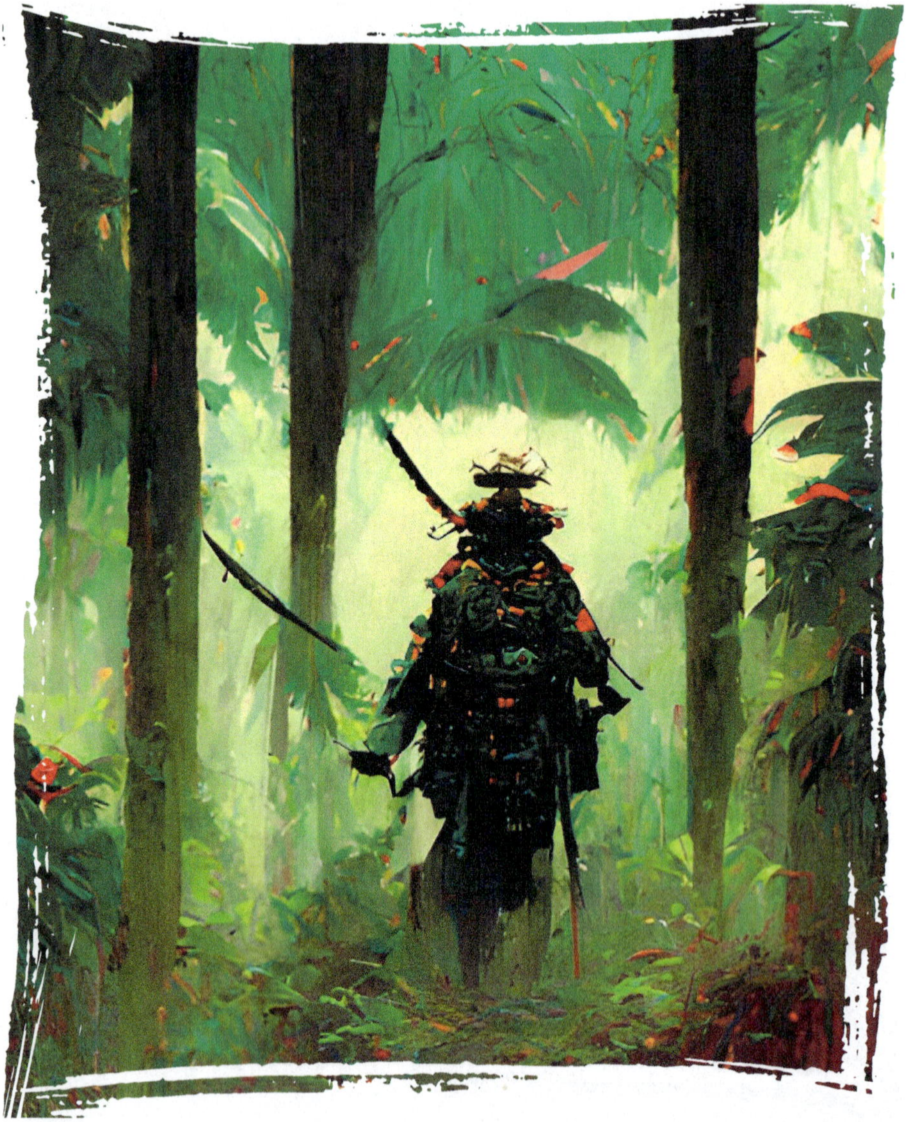

A description of the science of martial arts and analysis of the school founded by Musashi can be found in the Earth Manuscript. "As human beings it is essential for each of us to cultivate and polish our individual path.

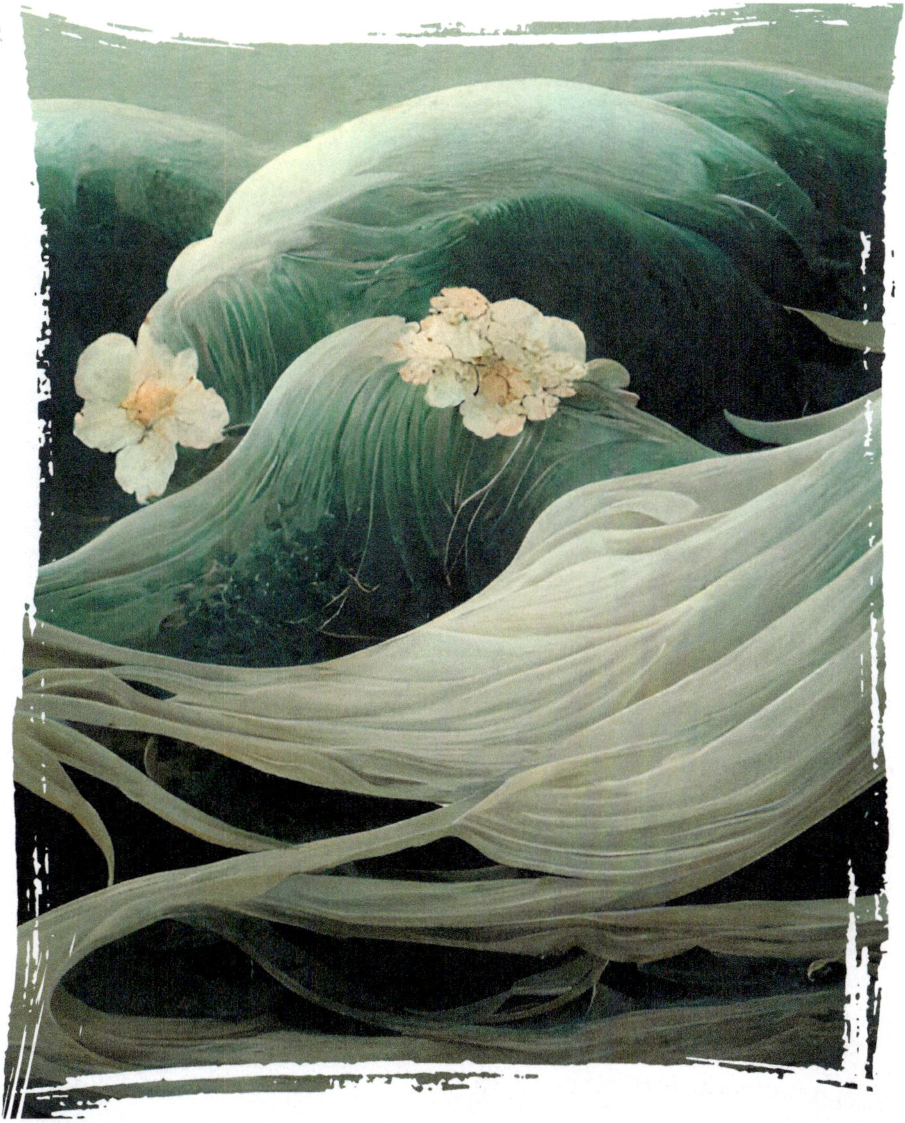

In the water manuscript, this element is taken as an essential point of reference to make the mind fluid. "Water adapts to the shape of the vessel, whether it is square or round, it can be a drop and it can also be the ocean."

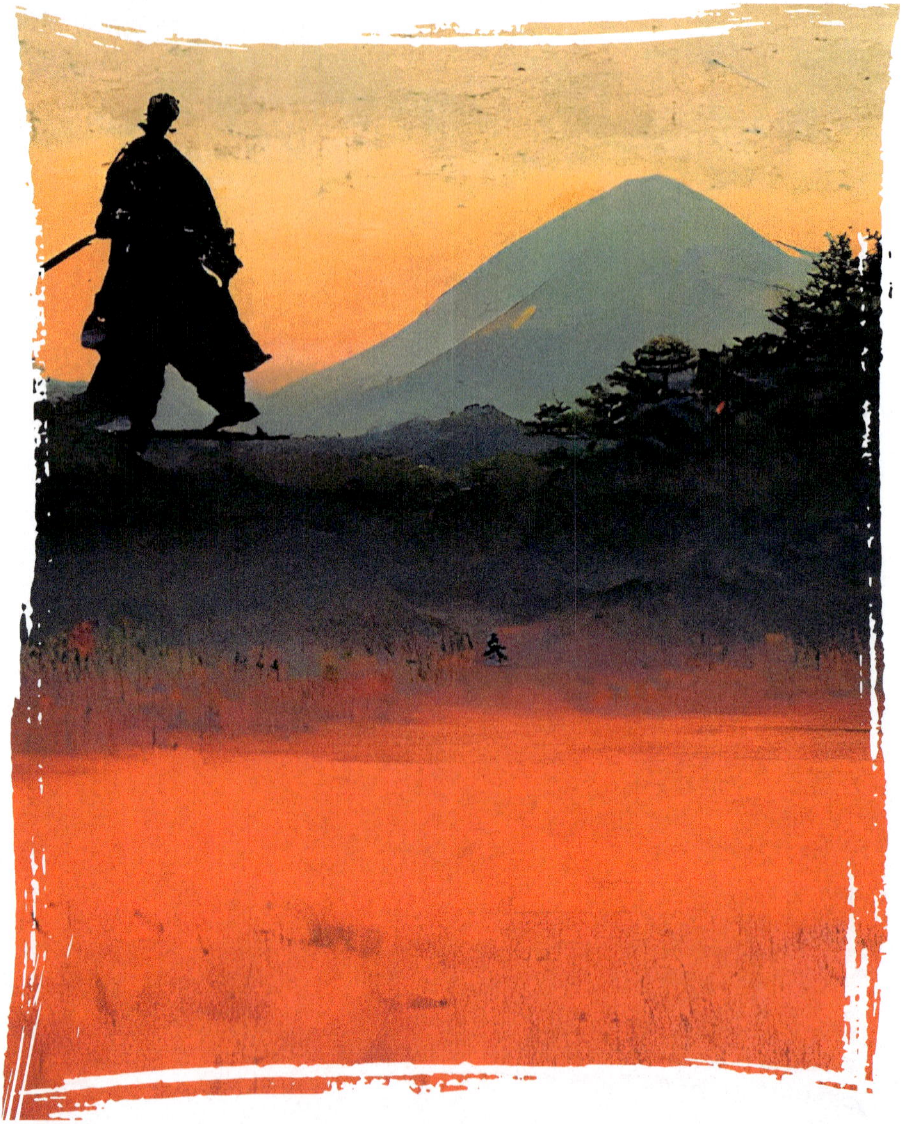

謹賀新年

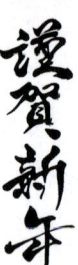

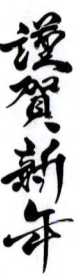

In the fire manuscript he writes about in battle "Harmony and disharmony are present in all forms of life. it is imperative to carefully distinguish between the rhythms of flowering and the rhythms of decay in each specific thing. ¨

謹賀新年

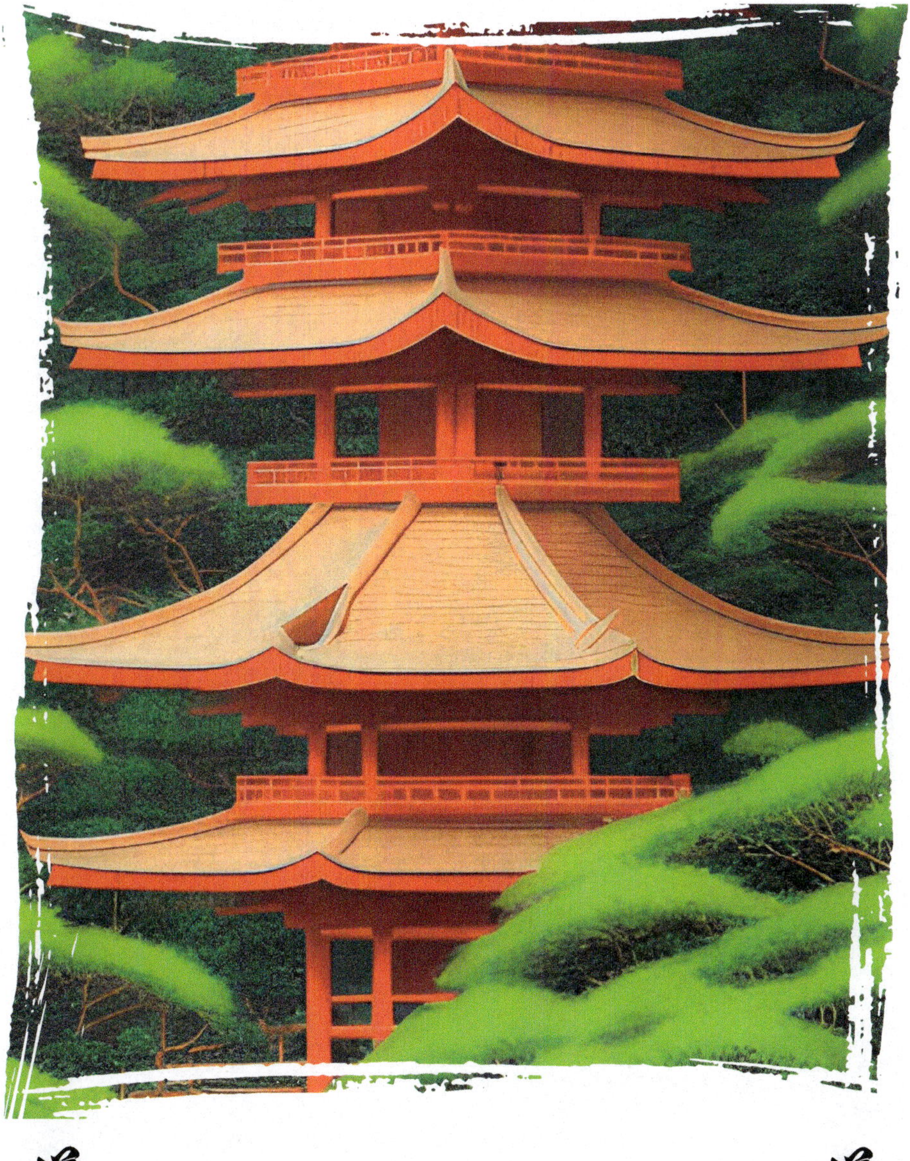

謹賀新年

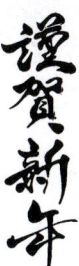

The air manuscript is dedicated to analyzing the various schools of martial arts that existed in other parts of Japan

謹賀新年

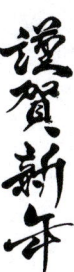

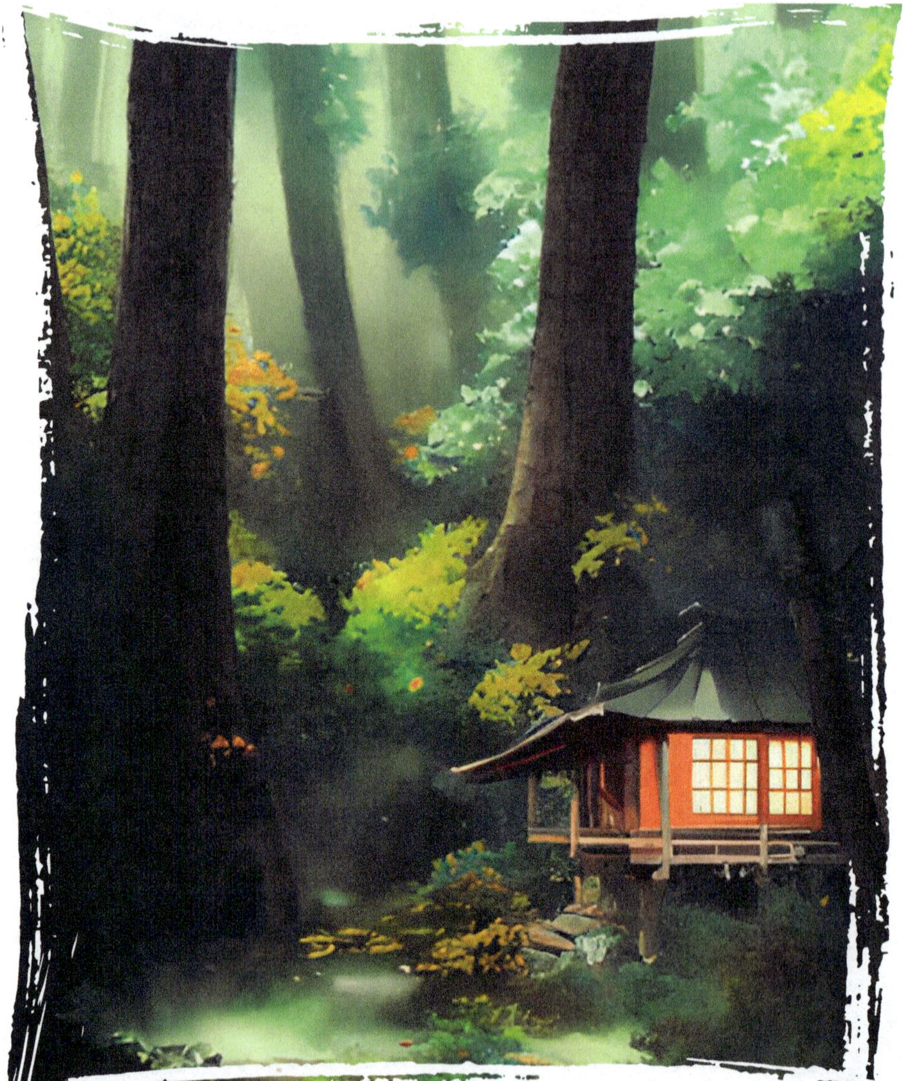

謹賀新年

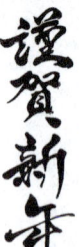

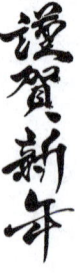

The last one is the emptiness manuscript where he writes about the natural entrance into the true way "Without any confusion of spirit, by polishing the mind and attention by sharpening the seeing eye and the seeing eye, one arrives at the real emptiness as the state where there is no darkness and the clouds of confusion have disappeared. ¨

謹賀新年

A week before he died, he wrote his second book Dokkodo, the path of solitude or the path that must be followed alone or the path of self-discipline consisting of 21 principles of life. These principles are naturally his particular way of understanding life from the context of his own warrior culture and some may not be foreign, Musashi himself said that there is more than one path to the top of the mountain, so we should not take them as immutable laws but as precepts that reveal an imperishable wisdom if we know how to see them with a view free of prejudices.

謹賀新年

**ACCEPT EVERYTHING
EXACTLY THE WAY IT
IS.**

1

謹賀新年

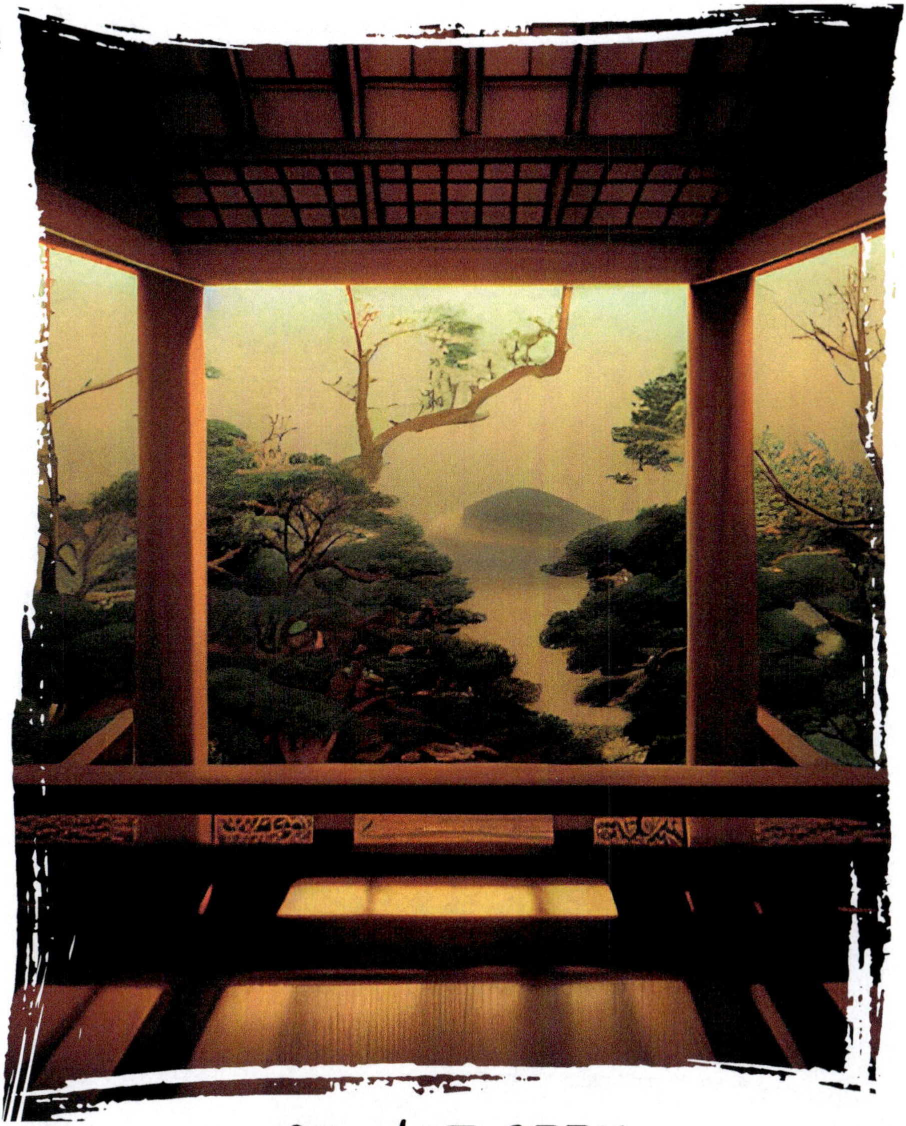

DO NOT SEEK
PLEASURE FOR THE
MERE CRAVING FOR
PLEASURE.

11

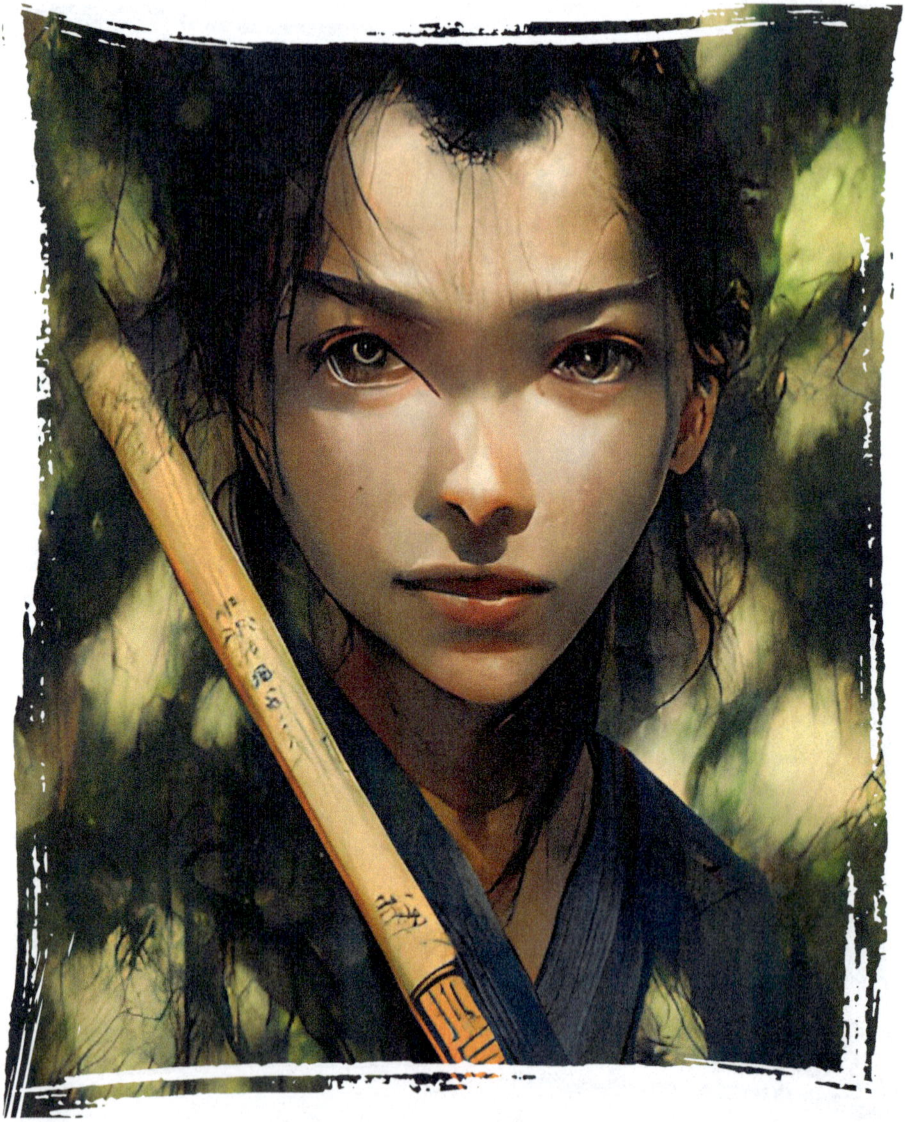

DO NOT DEPEND ON A PARTIAL FEELING UNDER ANY CIRCUMSTANCES, BE IMPARTIAL IN EVERYTHING, DO NOT BE CARRIED AWAY BY GREED.

III

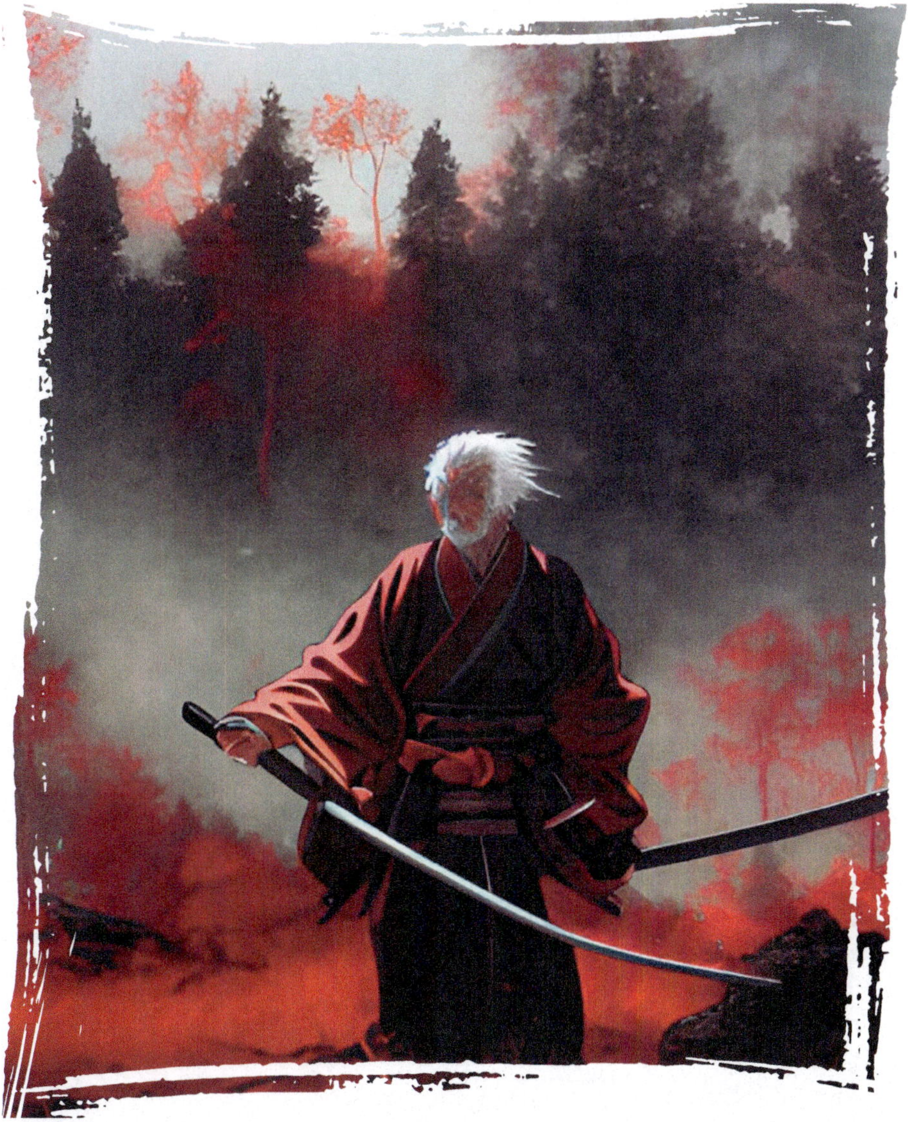

謹賀新年

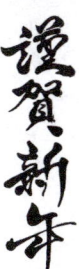

THINK LIGHTLY OF YOURSELF AND DEEPLY OF THE WORLD, DO NOT WORRY ABOUT SELFISH MATTERS.

IV

謹賀新年

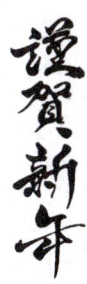

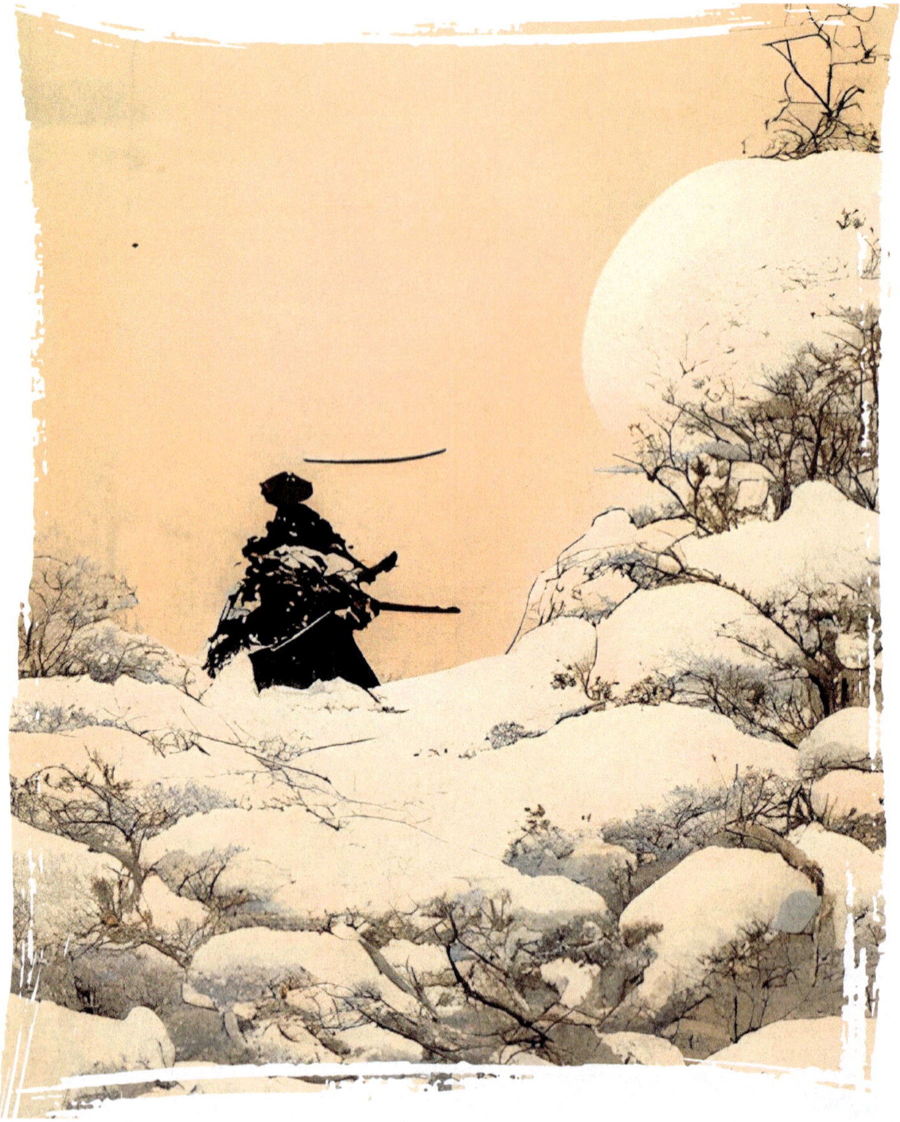

謹賀新年

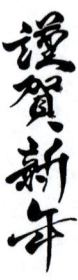

STAY SEPARATE FROM DESIRE
THROUGHOUT YOUR WHOLE LIFE.
V

謹賀新年

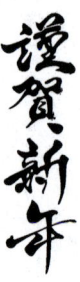

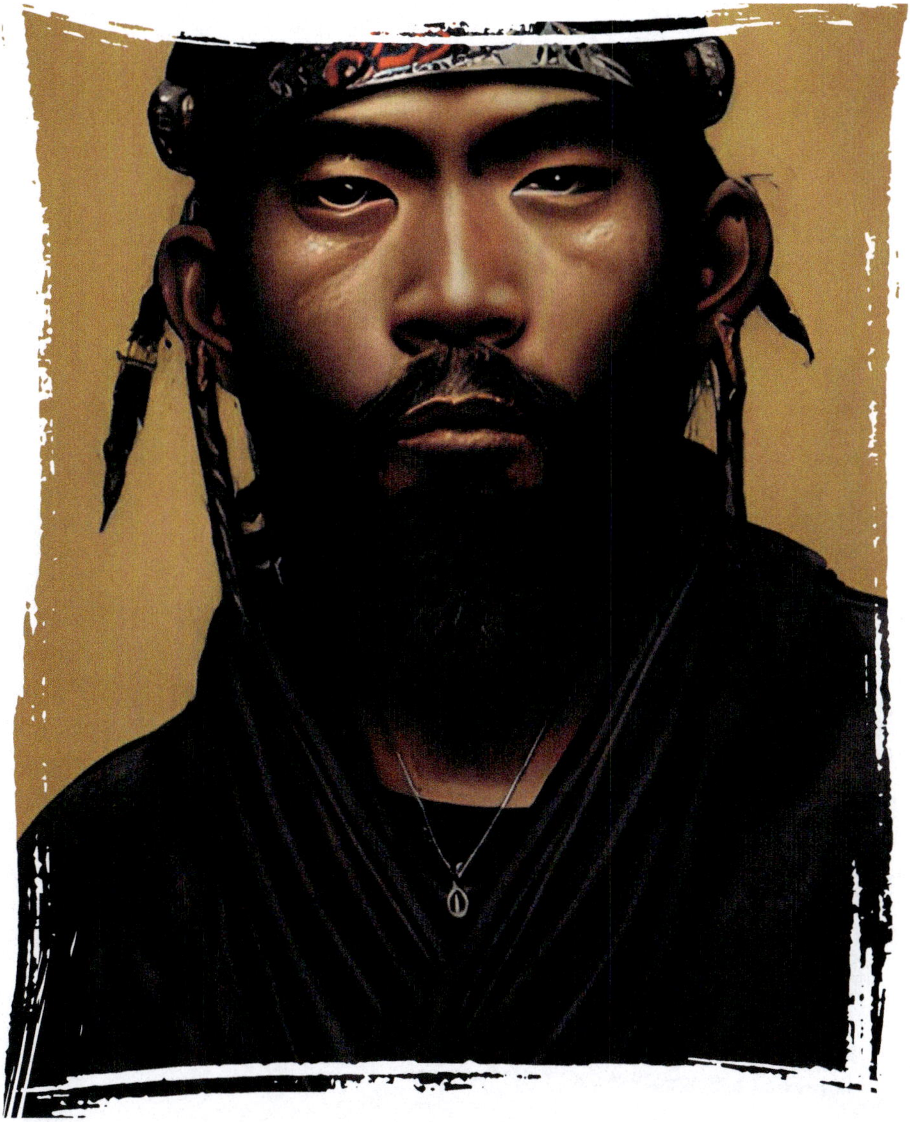

謹賀新年

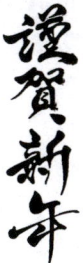

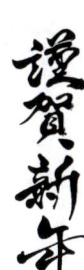

NEVER REGRET WHAT EXISTS, DO NOT HOLD GRUDGES OR ANIMOSITY TOWARDS YOURSELF OR TOWARDS OTHERS.

VI

謹賀新年

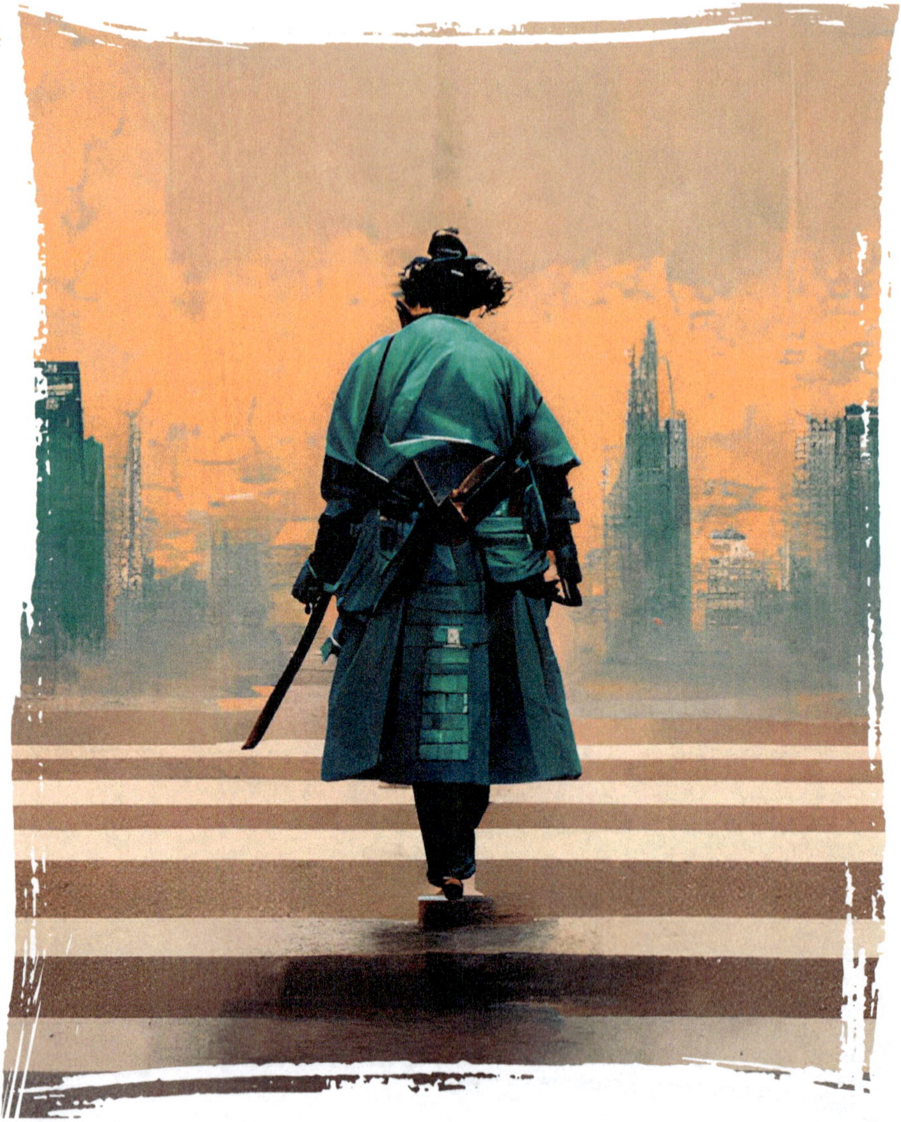

謹賀新年

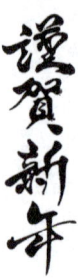

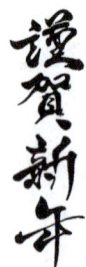

NEVER REGRET WHAT EXISTS, DO NOT HOLD GRUDGES OR ANIMOSITY TOWARDS YOURSELF OR TOWARDS OTHERS.

VII

謹賀新年

謹賀新年　　謹賀新年

NEVER BE SAD ABOUT A
SEPARATION.
VIII

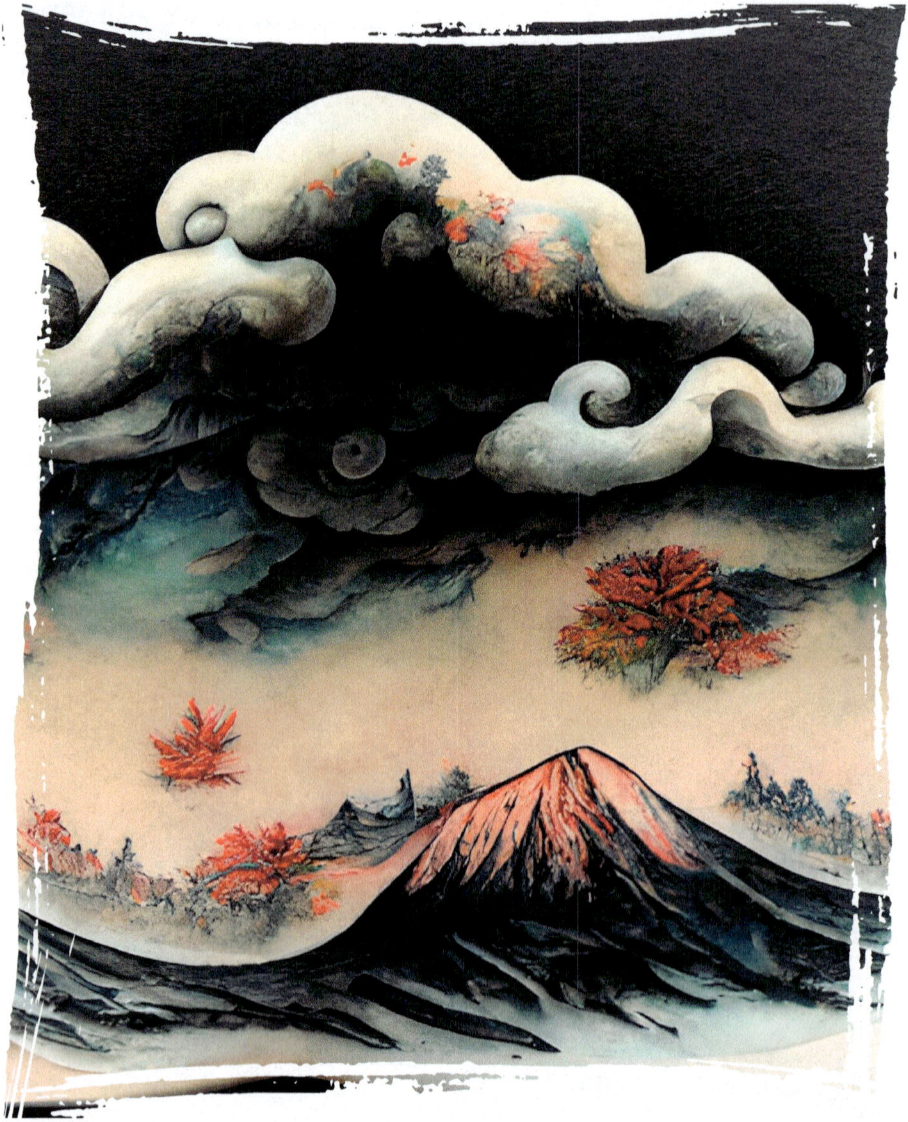

謹賀新年

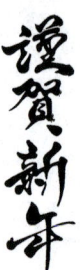

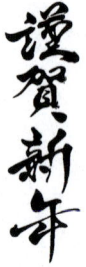

RESENTMENT AND COMPLAINTS TOWARDS YOURSELF OR OTHERS ARE NOT APPROPRIATE, NEVER BLAME ANYTHING.

IX

謹賀新年

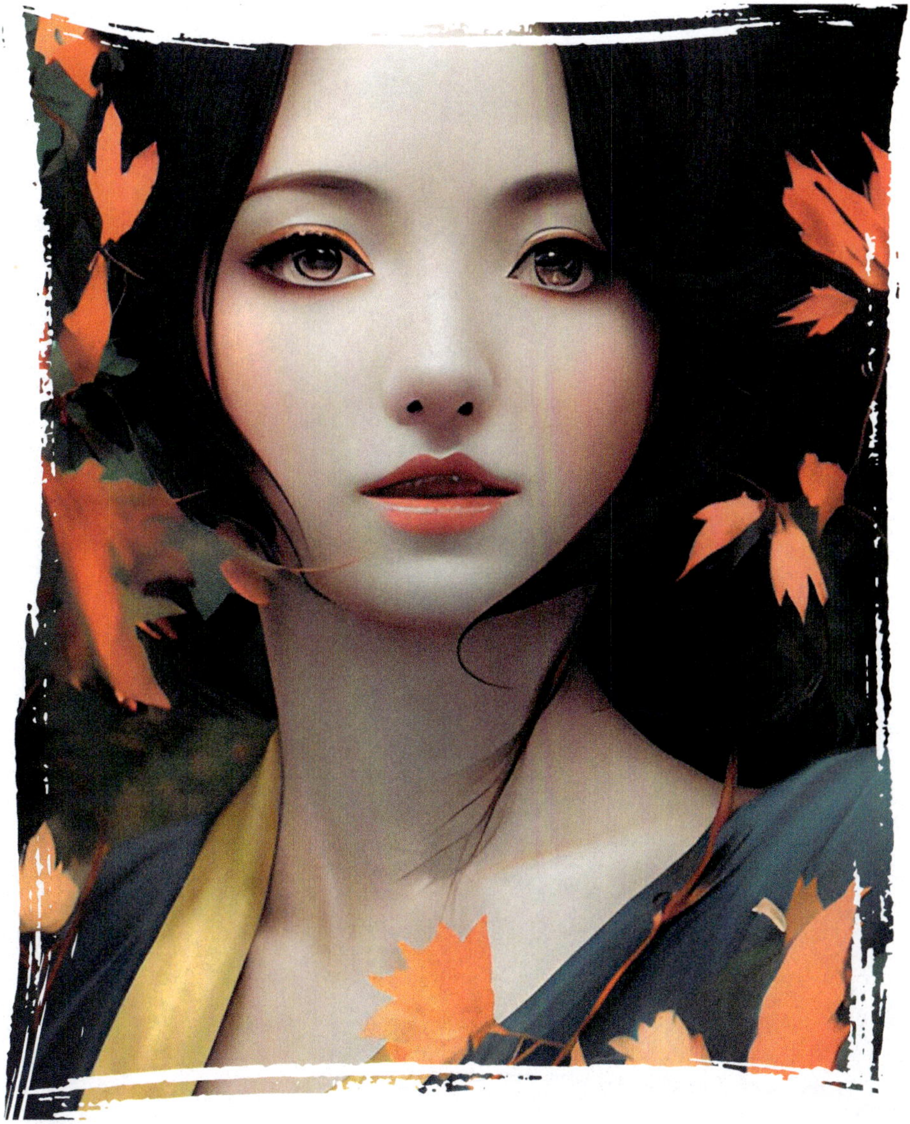

謹賀新年

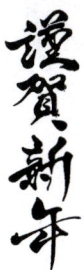

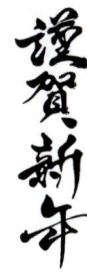

NEVER LET LUST GUIDE YOU,
DON'T BECOME A COWARD
BECAUSE OF THE BODY.
X

謹賀新年

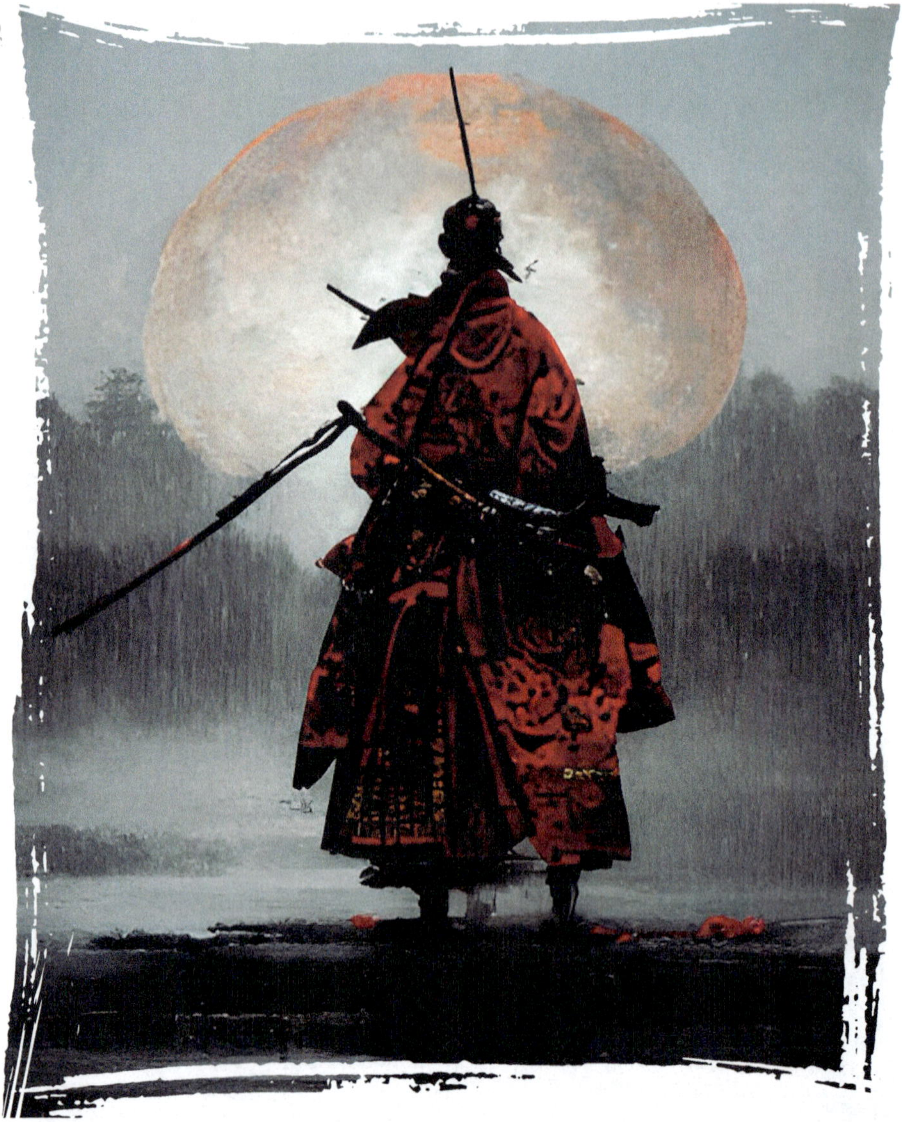

謹賀新年

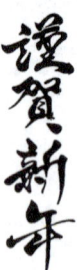

DO NOT HAVE PREFERENCES IN ANY THING LIKES AND DISLIKES DO NOT HAVE ANY.

XI

謹賀新年

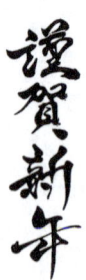

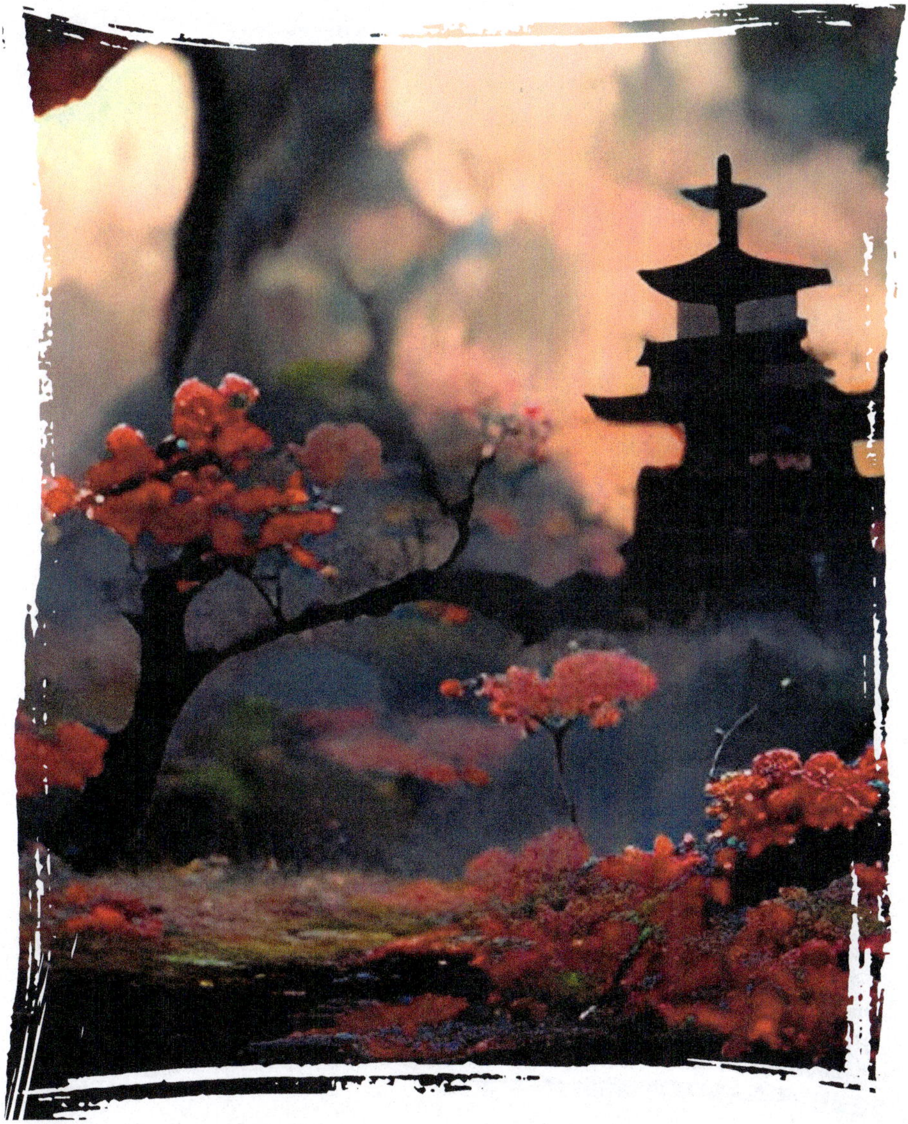

謹賀新年

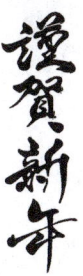

BE INDIFFERENT TO WHERE YOU LIVE, NO MATTER WHERE YOU LIVE, NEVER HAVE ANY OBJECTIONS AGAINST IT.

XII

謹賀新年

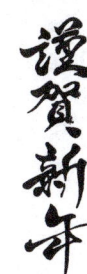

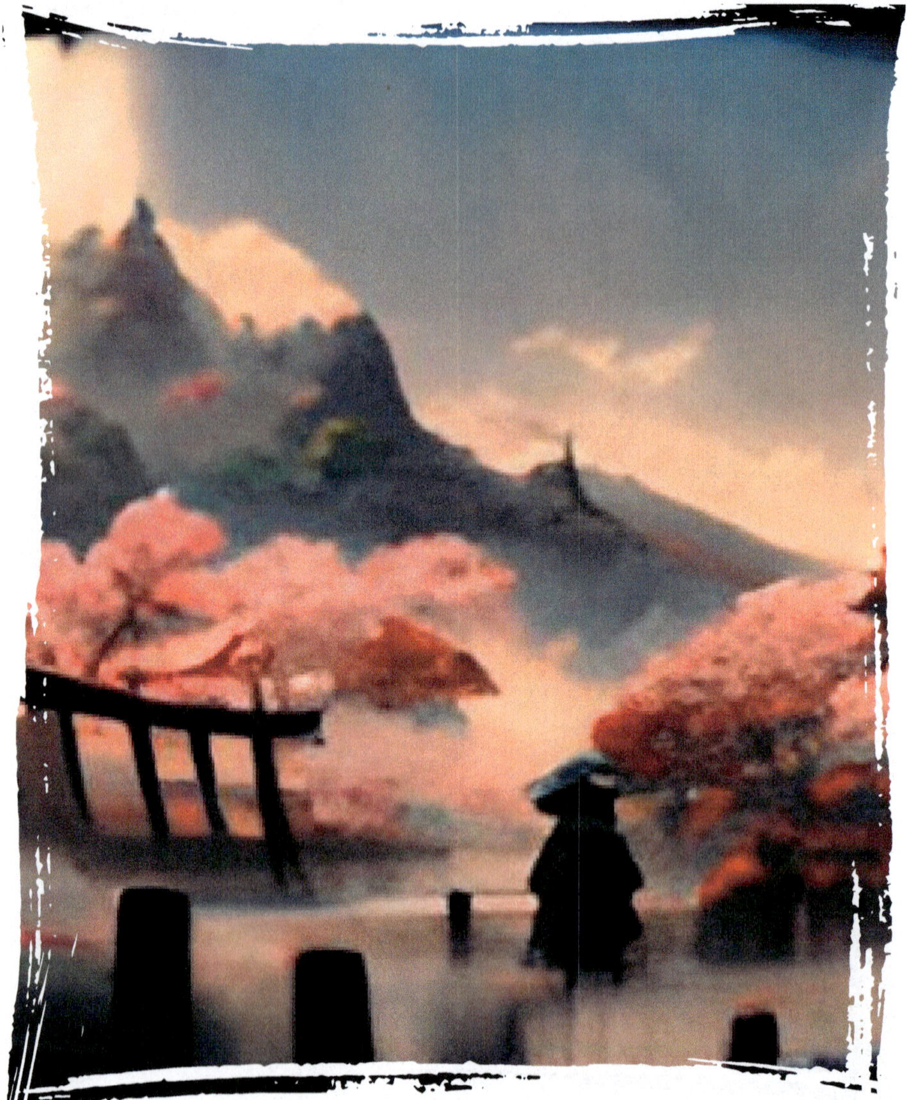

DON'T CHASE AFTER TRYING
GOOD FOOD, DON'T LOOK FOR
THE MOST REFINED DISHES TO
SATISFY THE BODY
XII + I

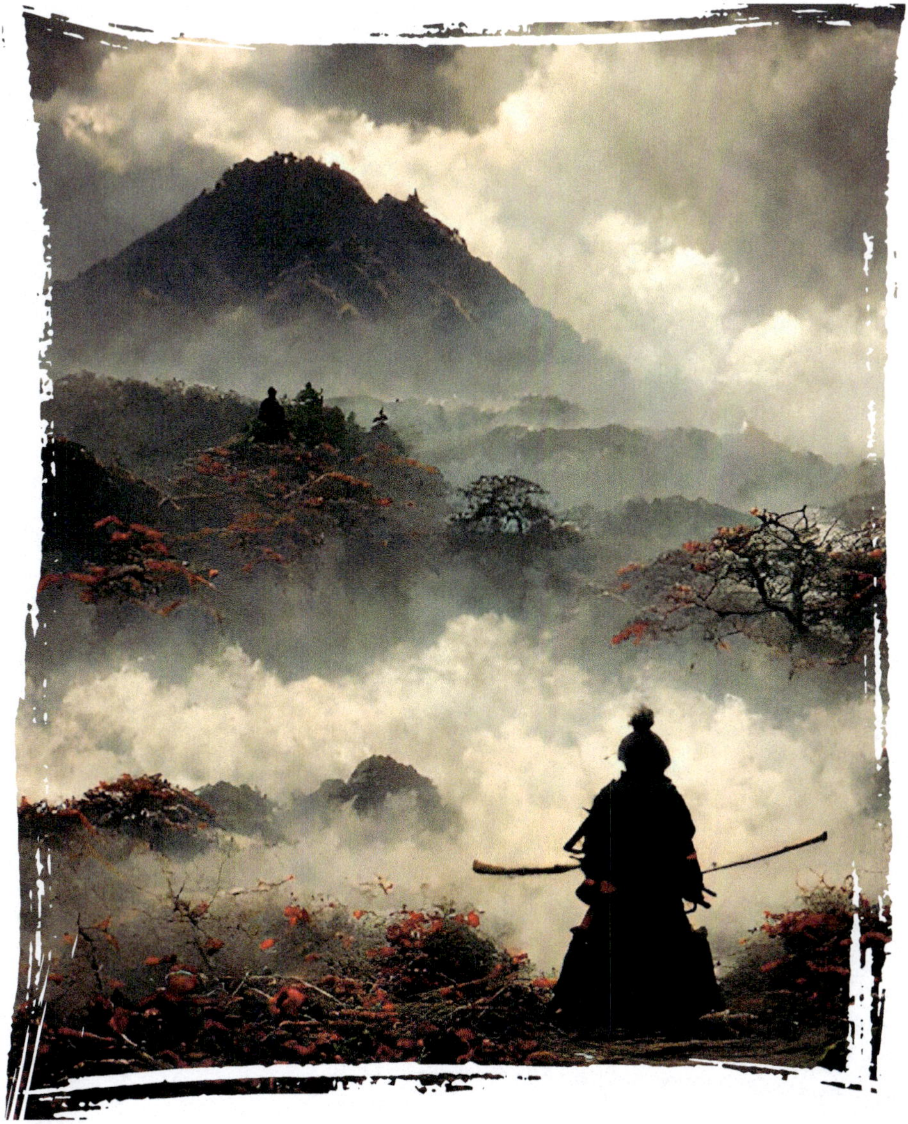

謹賀新年

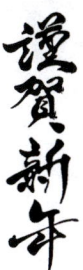

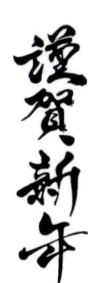

DON'T HOLD ON TO
POSSESSIONS YOU NO LONGER
NEED.
XIV

謹賀新年

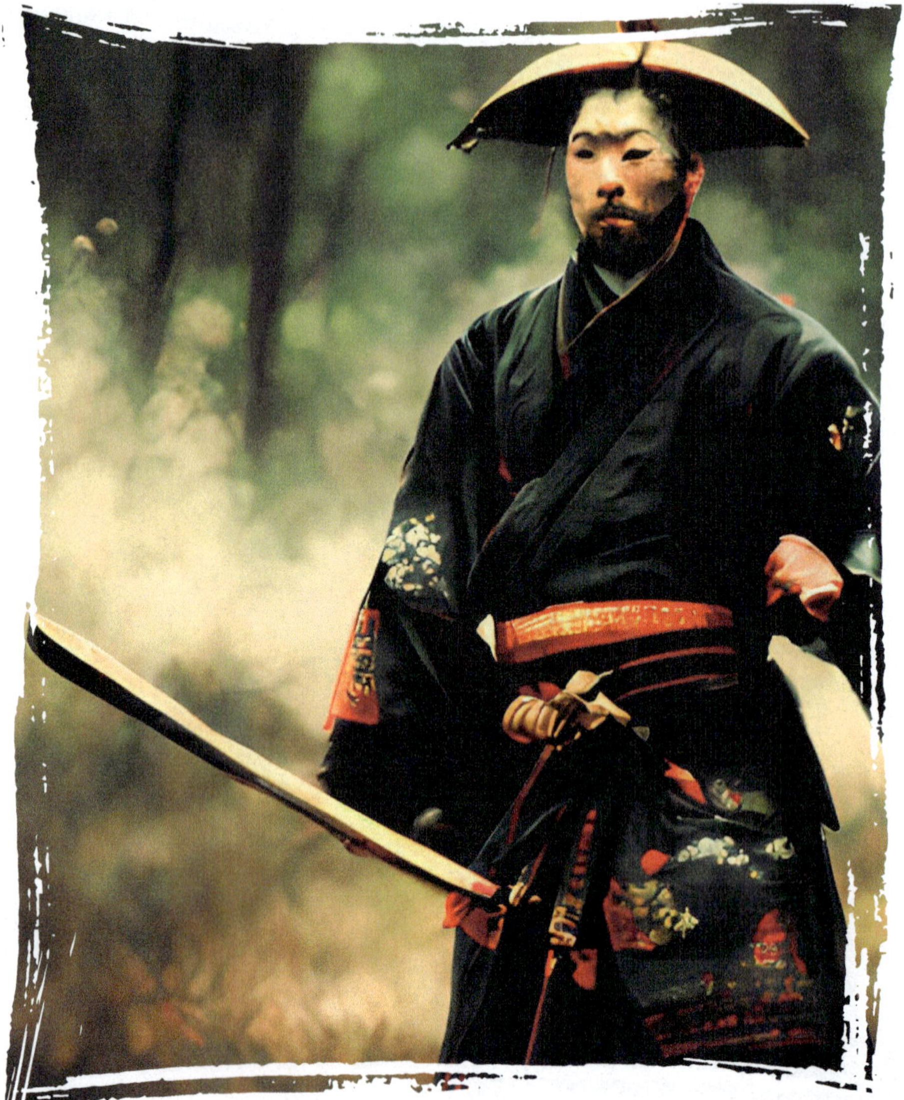

謹賀新年

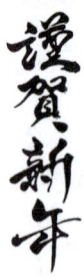

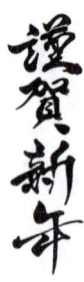

DO NOT ACT FOLLOWING
CUSTOMS OR SUPERSTITIONS.
XV

謹賀新年

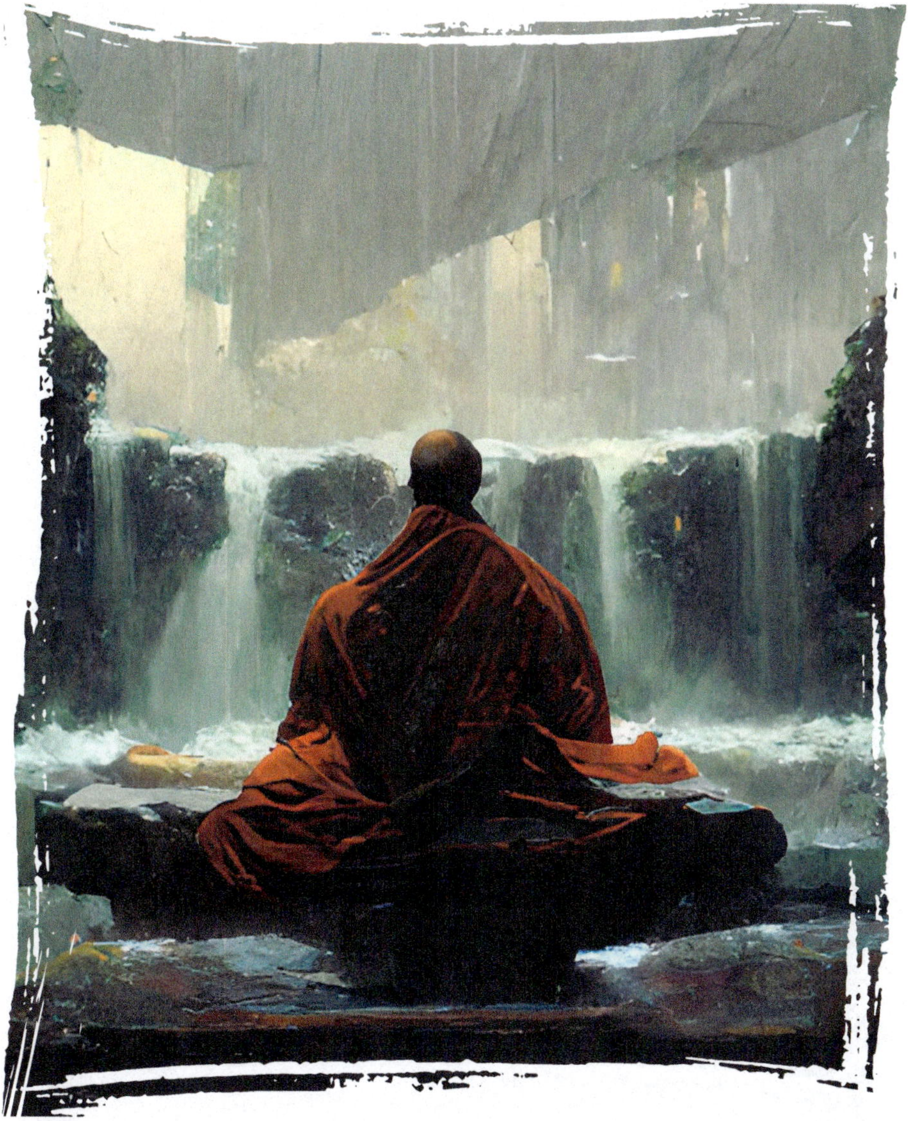

謹賀新年

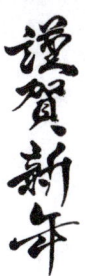

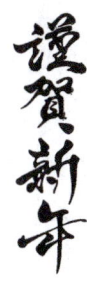

DO NOT COLLECT WEAPONS OR
PRACTICE WITH THEM BEYOND
WHAT IS USEFUL.
XVI

謹賀新年

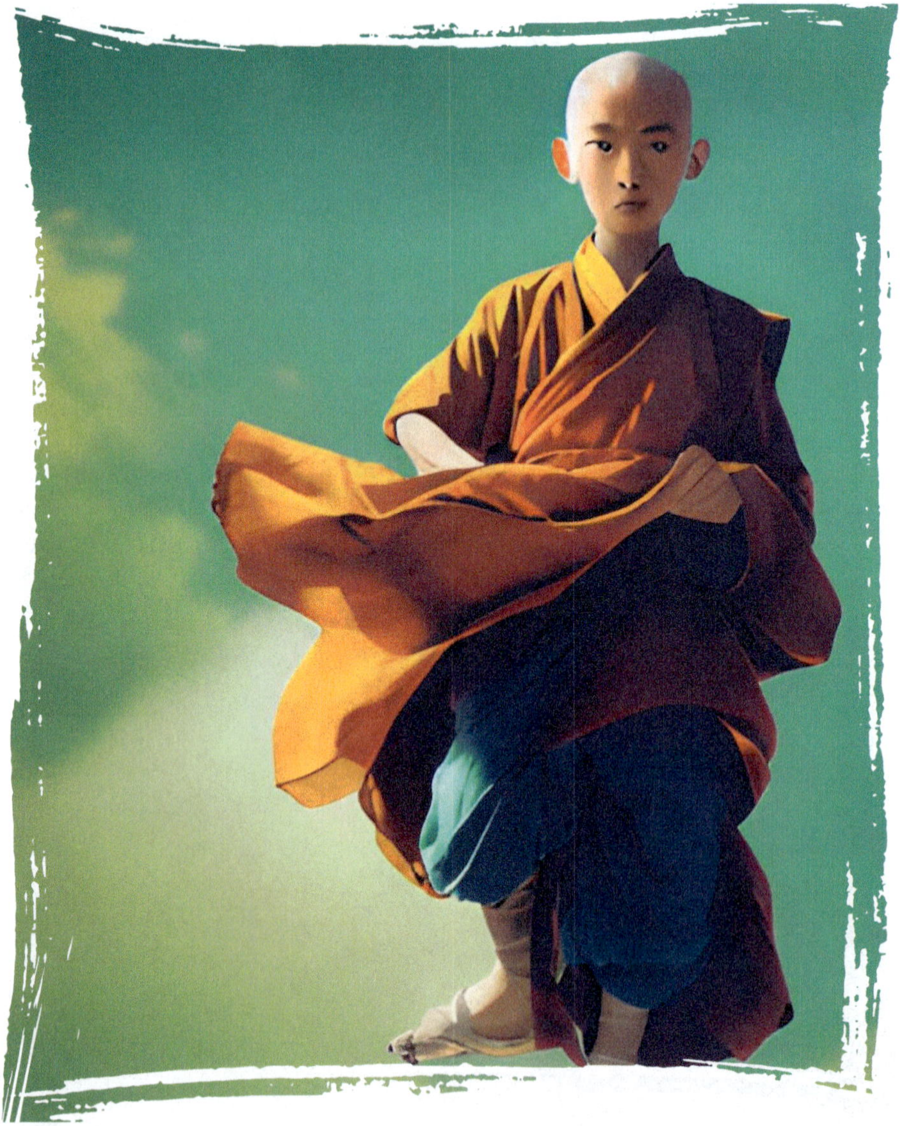

謹賀新年

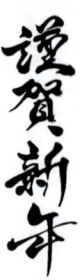

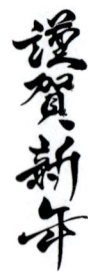

DO NOT FEAR DEATH,
CONSECRATE YOURSELF ENTIRELY
TO LIFE WITHOUT FEAR UNTIL
THE END.

XVII

謹賀新年

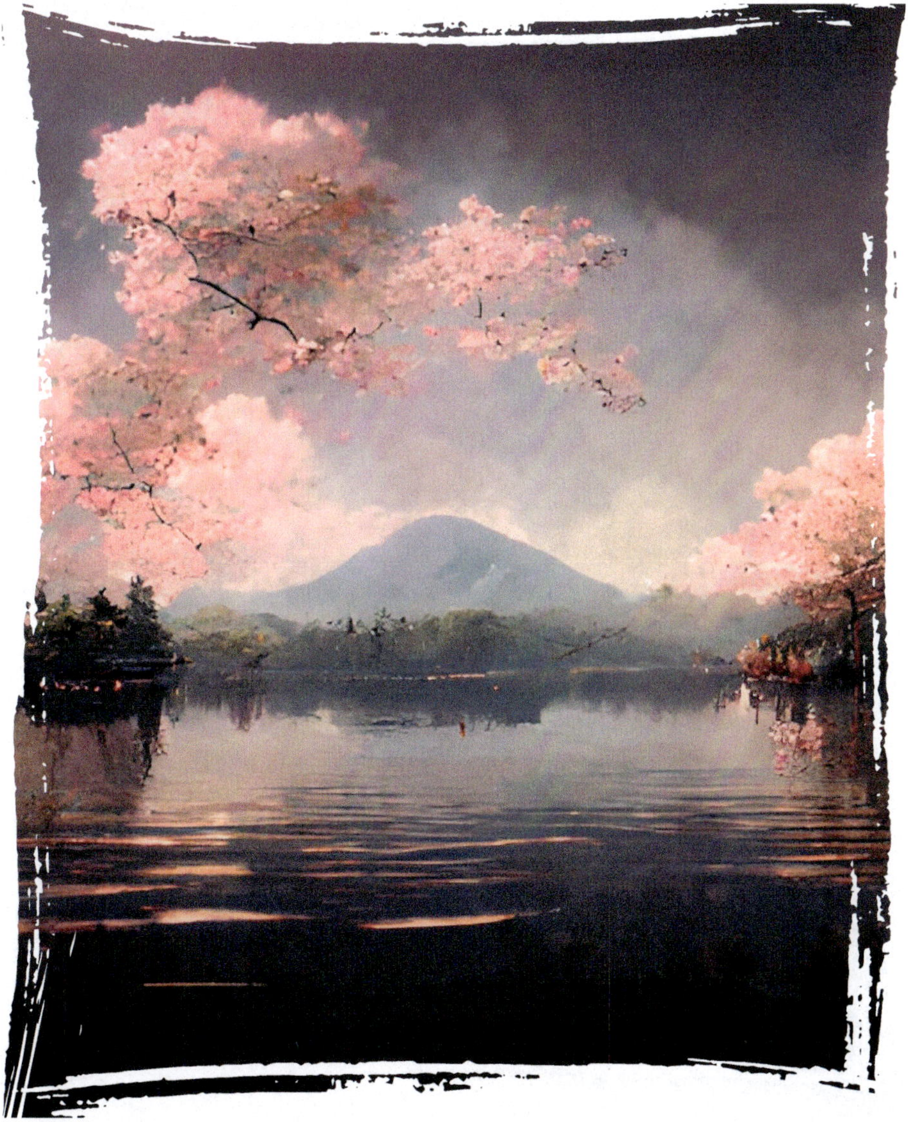

謹賀新年

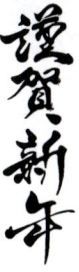

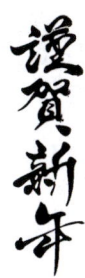

DO NOT SEEK TO OWN PROPERTY
OR FIEFDOMS IN YOUR OLD AGE.
XVIII

謹賀新年

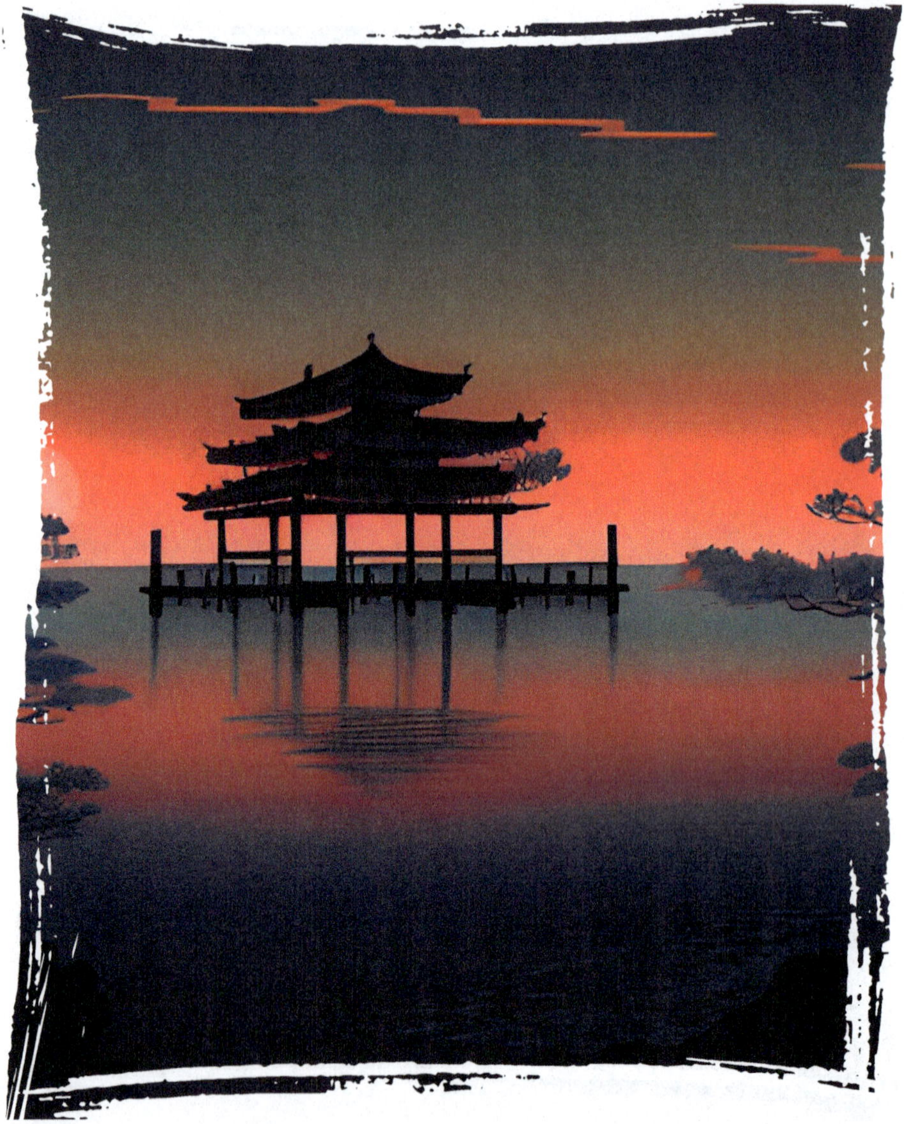

謹賀新年

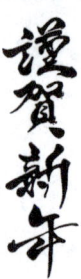

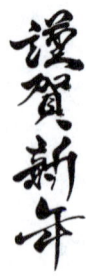

RESPECT BUDDHA AND THE GODS WITHOUT EXPECTING THEM TO COME TO YOUR AID. REVERE THEM, BUT DON'T THINK OF DEPENDING ON THEM.

XIX

謹賀新年

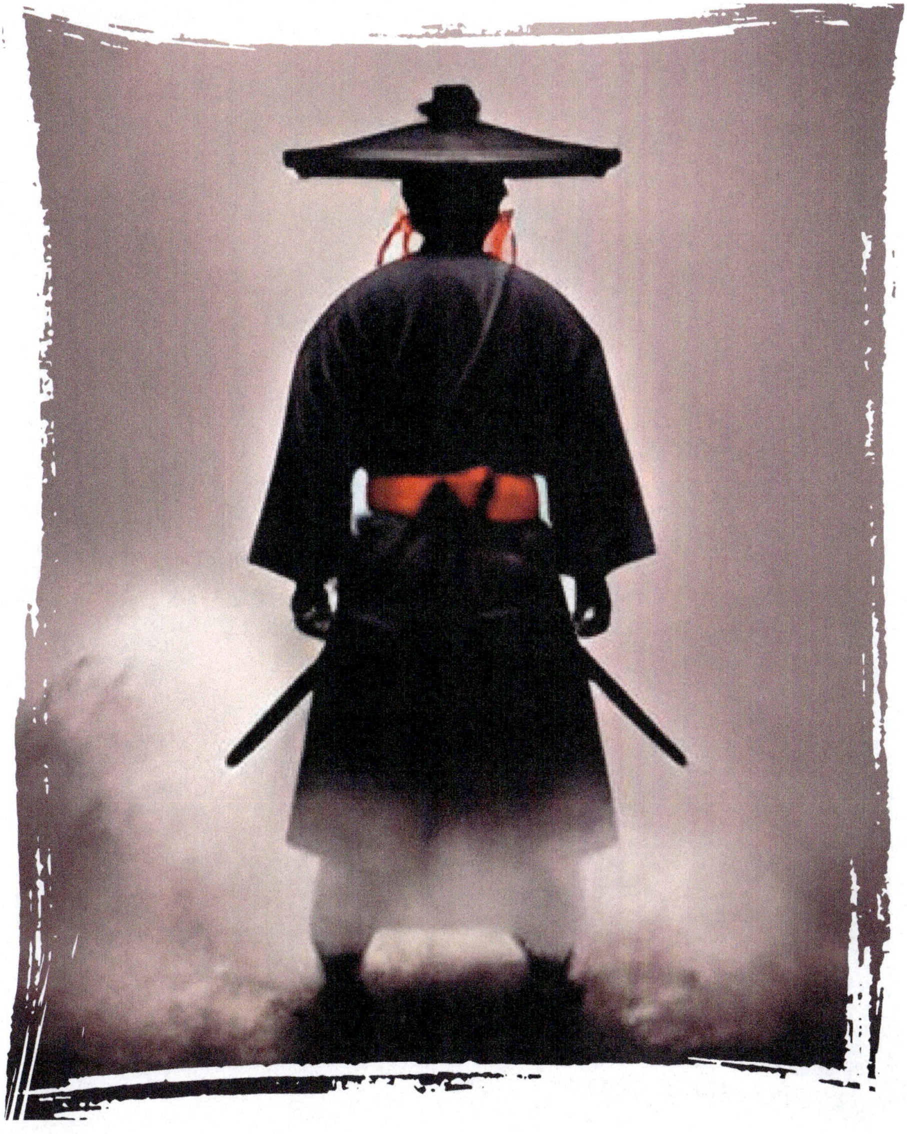

謹賀新年

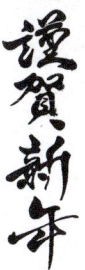

PRESERVE HONOR IN THE FACE
OF DEATH, IT IS BETTER TO DIE
HONORABLY THAN TO DISHONOR
YOUR GOOD NAME.

XX

謹賀新年

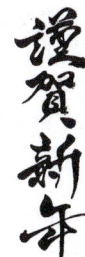

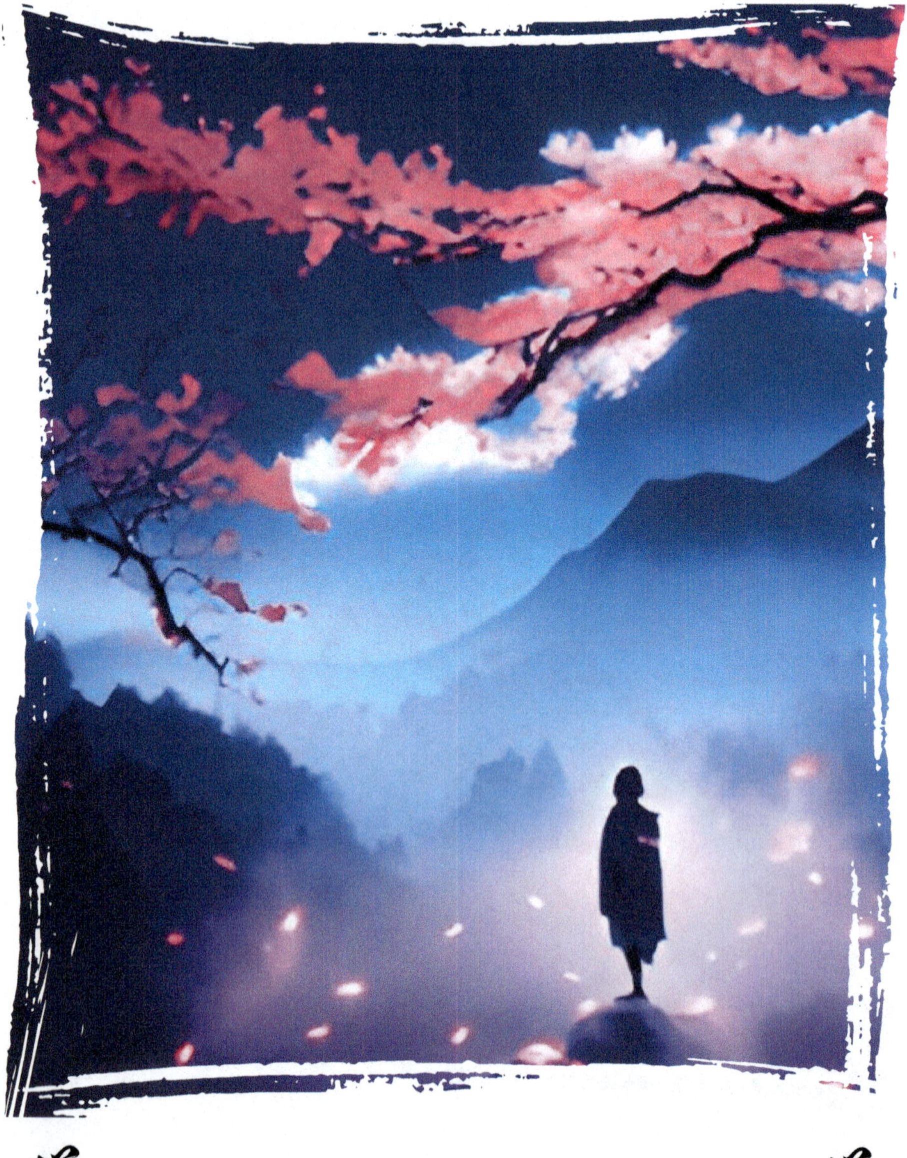

謹賀新年

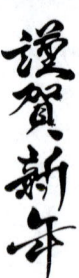

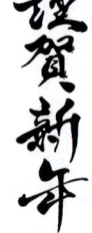

NEVER STRAY FROM THE PATH.
NEVER, NOT FOR A MOMENT,
NEITHER IN BODY NOR IN SOUL,
STRAY FROM THE PATH.

XXI

謹賀新年

NOTAS

NOTAS

NOTAS

NOTAS

NOTAS

NOTAS

NOTAS

NOTAS

NOTAS

NOTAS

NOTAS

NOTAS

NOTAS

NOTAS

NOTAS

NOTAS

NOTAS

NOTAS

NOTAS

NOTAS

NOTAS

NOTAS

NOTAS

NOTAS

NOTAS

NOTAS

Printed in Great Britain
by Amazon

27081201R00044